FA

FALLING

by

DEBBIE MOON

HONNO MODERN FICTION

Published by Honno
'Alisa Craig', Heol y Cawl, Dinas Powys
South Glamorgan, Wales, CF6 4AH

ISBN 1 870206 61 4

Published with the financial support of the Arts Council of Wales

The author would like to thank Patricia Duncker for all her help in developing and editing the text.

Cover design and photograph by Jo Mazelis

Author photograph by Kate Wright and Matt Jarvis

Typeset and printed in Wales by
Gwasg Dinefwr, Llandybïe.

She was falling.

Looking down from here, it must be eighty or ninety storeys to the ground. There was something wrong with her left arm, a weakness, a pain, perhaps broken, but she didn't remember –

Jude didn't remember.

For someone in her profession, that was unusual. She made a habit of not forgetting. Oh, she could remember her name, address, all the flotsam that would have gone in standard amnesia. But not how she'd got here.

You'd have thought that falling to your death was pretty memorable.

Her ears popped. She was cold; deep, biting cold, numbing her thoughts, sandpapering her bare arms. There was light, light from the windows, light from the sky, but no shapes. Just blurs that spilled from her vision before she could force them into recognisable shapes.

Her limbs swam against the air rush, thrashing for traction, and she couldn't stop them. She didn't have time to try.

She needed to concentrate.

She'd ReTraced her way out of bad situations before: from in front of the barrel of a gun; back ten minutes to unsay the words that had led her there, or to take a different short-cut, a later train; remake a fatal decision with the benefit of hind-sight. Tracing the different permutations of her tangled life to find the best course of action, like some kid on an arcade game, using her limitless lives to test out each option, each risk, until she understood the pattern.

She was a ReTracer. That was what she did.

Why should this be any different?

Opening herself to the tangled skeins of time, Jude Re-Traced.

ONE

Club Andro, Midnight

And the party was in full swing.

Jude liked Club Andro, though jumping straight in like this was a shock – straight into synthetic perfumes and sweat and the heartbeat thump of defiantly retro acoustic reggae-rock. The cold metal curve of the bar dug into her back; jostling her from the side, the generous rear end of a girl in leather, bent over a table to offer something illegal to a group of startled tourists who'd obviously misread the guidebook.

The video headlines – NEW SEX SCANDAL ROCKS EURO-PARLIAMENT – didn't offer any clues as to which garbled, dissolute night of the early 21st century she'd Re-Traced her way back to. Neither did the homogenised fashion sense of the clientele; leather or fluorescent denim for the women, garish synthetics and heavy rogue on the men. Could have been any night in the past ten years.

Well. No rush. She could spend as much time as she liked in her past, and she'd return to her present-time body at the instant she'd left it. In the present, time was standing still. And she was hot and thirsty and restless – that defocused hyperactivity that drives you out onto the streets after dark, just to breathe in the night and consider the city spread out before you, yours for the taking.

And somewhere here, she'd find the key to her present-time dilemma, and change it, and everything would be fine.

Extricating herself from the leather-clad girl, Jude edged along the bar a little and took a look around.

It was tourist night. Big parties in from the army bases or the Hursts, to paddle in the shallows of big city decadence. They stood out a mile. Tourists wore Marilyns or Deans and thought they were fashionable. Tourists had popular catalogue partials – River Phoenix cheekbones or Van Damme pecs perched uneasily on their womb-bred bodies. She imagined them picking sections from the displays in the biotech clinics; one of these and one of those, and I must have what Eloise had, all the girls are talking about it . . .

Tourists looked like Drossers. No style, no brain, no-hopers.

Fumbling with the Tequila pump, Fitch, the gamine Korean barmaid, looked Jude over and grimaced. No way to tell what she was mouthing, not over the final chorus of *My Baby Bought A New Face (And Left Me Feeling Blue)*, but Jude could guess.

Something along the lines of, 'How did you get in here dressed like that?'

No, she wasn't really androj enough for Club Andro, not even in her treasured reproduction velvet frockcoat. You dressed big for Club Andro; big, loud, and in direct opposition to whatever gender you were wearing that week. Or you broke the rules and hoped to be admitted as that night's fashion casualty, there for the beautiful people to smirk at.

Fitch shook her head, as disgusted by the doorman's negligence as Jude's lack of taste. In the warm yellow light behind the bar, she looked almost childlike, fragile and innocent. Jude blew her a kiss and for a moment, she almost looked like she was blushing.

They were friends, then. A lot more than friends, of course; but looking back, friends was the important part. That set a minimum on how far she'd slipped back. Maybe if she could drag Fitch away from the bar for a moment, she could wheedle some solid information out of her.

The leather-clad girl had finished frightening the tourists, who were casting longing looks towards the door. As Jude eased past, she spread a double handful of coloured injectors before her, smiling crookedly. 'Wanna trip? Safest on the planet.'

Turning away from a sudden flare of strobe light, Jude shook her head. 'No thanks,' she yelled above the thrash-metal intro for the night's first act: bioengineered hermaphrodites, performing something that might loosely be considered dancing. 'I'm not wired for it.'

The girl studied her face for a moment, puzzled. 'Wired' was a throwback to an older and altogether cruder technology, but it was the standard term. More likely, the mere idea of someone frequenting Club Andro in their own unaltered birth body had shocked her into paralysis.

And led her to one inescapable conclusion.

'You're a cop.'

Jude shook her head. Heads were already turning. 'I'm a ReTracer,' she yelled, hoarse with dry ice and annoyance. 'A ReTracer. Don't you read the newspapers?'

Someone screamed an inaudible introduction over the thrash and the static, and the leather-girl, finally understanding, wrinkled her nose in contempt and turned away. Government employees with bizarre time-travelling powers obviously didn't rate highly in her world order, but at least they were better than cops.

The crowd to her left parted and Jude seized her chance. With the slick expertise of the experienced clubber, she elbowed her way through an argument, around an amorous clinch, and out into what passed for a clear space.

'Woah, Judey-baby,' the female at the nearest table simpered, fluttering eyelashes that masked puppy-dog eyes green as grass. 'Long time, no see, huh?'

Jude studied the clubber's long, fine-boned face in the treacherous light. There were familiar things: the last traces of a heavier jaw line, the habitual slight sag at the corners of a new, perfect mouth. All the little clues you learned to look for, when a trip to the clinic was as routine as a new pair of shoes and even your dearest friends couldn't be counted upon to look the same way twice.

'Miyahara?'

'The very same,' the soft female mouth replied. The voice was perfect – pleasant register, trace of a Scandinavian accent, very fashionable. But underneath, a quick ear could still pick out the mannered politeness of garbled Japanese ancestry. 'How do you like my latest?'

Miyahara had always been overly fond of stereotypes and his latest incarnation was pure Fantasy Swedish Blond; golden curls to her waist, legs to her armpits, breasts that could have suckled an entire orphanage. It reminded her of the first bioteched porn stars; of furtive magazine reading under the bedclothes, as much amused as aroused.

Always the same. Give them the chance to be anything, and they all want to look the same. It's like the world being packed with dirt-cheap designer clothing and all anyone wants to wear are plastic sandals and pastel-blue jogging outfits.

She still hadn't answered his question. 'It's – extraordinary.'

'You're most kind. Won't you join me?'

She didn't remember having met Miyahara in this modification before – and it was pretty memorable. They could have missed each other a dozen times, any night of the week, in the swirling currents of humanity that filled Club Andro. But tonight, they hadn't.

That felt significant, and significance was exactly what she was looking for.

Jude eased herself into the chair opposite – bolted down and a tight fit, a reminder to the clientele that only the thin and the beautiful were welcome here – and signalled a passing waiterette. 'Scotch and soda,' she yelled and, to Miyahara, 'You look taller.'

'Eleven centimetres,' Miyahara beamed, perfect teeth fluorescing in the insistent pulse of UV. 'It cost. And it hurt.'

The waiterette, bioteched to the five-foot South American tribal model that had become the club's trademark, sniffed dismissively and flounced off through the crowd, using her elbows to clear a path while balancing a tray in each hand.

'Cute.' Miyahara watched her virtually naked buttocks vanish into the heaving ranks of leather and silk. 'I've heard that the waiterettes are equipped both ways, you know.'

'Yeah?' Jude murmured, distracted by a scuffle at the door. Metal claws flashed in a pulse of green light; someone screamed and the security staff waded in, the crowd closing nonchalantly around them as they quietened the brawlers with heavily reinforced fists.

'But then, who isn't these days?' Miyahara yawned, hiding his mouth with the back of one long-nailed hand. 'You should really get with the action. Oh. Of course. You can't.'

Jude's turn to yawn. They had this conversation every time they met. Miyahara had even given up allowing her time to rise to the bait before ploughing on. 'ReTracers don't get to change. Just in case they damage that wonderful genetic accident that –'

'Button it, Miyahara. Some of us don't actually want to look like a reject from the Keep It Up All Night Channel.'

Miyahara spared her a smile that could have cut glass. 'Bio-engineering's not all it's cracked up to be, you know. Keeping up with the neighbours. The pressure. And frankly, I'm growing a little jaded. There are only so many permutations, even in the black market clinics. Though animal-human hybrids are looking quite promising . . .'

Images from old movies swam behind Jude's eyelids; impractically dressed women fainting as slavering creatures pawed at the windows.

'You want to be careful who you let loose on your genes, Miyahara. Some of the stories I've heard . . .'

'Heard them,' the female declared, with a dismissive wave of one hand. Ill-cut diamonds glittered across his knuckles. 'And you shouldn't believe everything you read. Trust me, I should know. I invent most of it.'

The waiterette returned with the scotch, and Jude tucked a banknote into her synthetic snakeskin loincloth. The girl flashed a false smile, moaning and wriggling in affected arousal, the house style, then leant close to murmur, 'Fitch wants to see you. Room Eight, half an hour.'

'I'll be there.'

The thrash-metal had subsided into a gut-vibrating percussive thumping. Finding themselves largely ignored, the dance troupe were in retreat, pausing only to lap-dance the occasional customer drunk enough to tip for what most of the clientele would have done for free.

'So,' Miyahara said casually, leaning back in his seat, 'how is the saving-the-world business these days?'

'It pays the bills.'

'Saved anyone famous recently? C'mon, just an off the record rumour, no one's going to trace it to you.'

Jude couldn't quite repress a smile. 'And what if I did? Let's say I ReTrace to save the President of Outer Mongolia from an assassin, have the guy arrested as he enters the concert hall instead. By definition, there was no assassination attempt. And even your gutter press rag isn't so desperate that it'll report non-events.'

'Okay.' The female nodded, unfazed. 'So, what about the inside story on bodyguarding the rich and famous? You have to follow them around, right? So you'll be in the right place to jump back to if anything happens. You must have seen a few things in your time. Sex, drugs, all the usual – and the less usual. I heard Sandra Rose had her vocal chords reshaped to the same dimensions as Elvis's, you got anything on that?'

Jude downed her scotch. She was beginning to get the feeling that, whatever she'd come back here to fix, it had nothing to do with Miyahara.

'If I spot any starlets with their pants down, I'll give you a call. Right now, I have to visit the freshening room.'

'I could come and, ah, give you a hand.' Miyahara smiled up at her. 'Don't say you aren't curious.'

'It's not that, Miya.' A sudden influx of rowdy girls in short pants had started a crowd current, and she took advantage of it, letting the shifting patterns of movement carry them apart. 'You should know by now. I never did go for blondes.'

Any attempt to divide the freshening rooms into ladies and gents had long since been abandoned, and inside clubbers of every conceivable gender were fighting for mirror space. Posturing abandoned, they jostled and elbowed, leaning close to the badly-lit glass to powder and paint with fierce self-absorption.

Jude sighed and headed for the cubicles.

The things you had to do to hear reliable gossip these days.

In a competitive market that catered for every taste, Club Andro thrived on its reputation for gossip. You wanted the latest scandal from New Hollywood, or good bets for your share portfolio, or just about anything else, this was the place to come.

Rumour had it that Leonarda, the gone-to-seed porn actress who'd founded the place with her last libel award, paid industry insiders hard cash to break their rumours here first. Just to preserve the club's reputation. You could spot her contacts, people maintained, by the overacted secrecy and the stage whispers. Now everyone who wanted to look important enough to be paid for their info sat hamming it up in corners, muttering just a little too loud and scowling at the tourists.

It tended to make for an interesting evening.

The facilities reeked of cheap perfume, and by the time she'd checked the hidden pockets of her coat – wads of various currencies, a fresh battery in the shock-net sewn into the velvet, painkillers and two trank darts, all present and correct – Jude was finding it hard to breathe.

How anyone ever survived an assignation in here without asphyxiating, she'd never know. Maybe that explained some of the more interesting noises coming from adjacent cubicles.

Buttoning the black cotton shirt defensively to the collar, Jude wrenched the cubicle door open and took two steps into the chaos.

'We was beginning to think,' a soft voice said into her ear, 'that you have a weak bladder.'

Turning her head just enough to look MultiLegion in the eye, Jude tried a thin smile.

She knew exactly when she was now.

And she was in deep shit.

'MultiLegion –'

Echoing the words inside her head, words she remembered speaking, when was it? Must have been early November last year, the streets had been sugared with frost when they went out to the alley . . .

Not the alley. Don't think about the alley, not yet. Concentrate on the present, on re-enacting everything just right, on looking for the one tiny thing to change.

Staring into eyes the colour of blood, Jude croaked, 'Whoever it is sent you, whatever they paid, GenoBond will pay you double.'

Drawing himself up to his full seven-and-a-half feet, MultiLegion shook his huge, heavy head. Lank dreadlocks writhed across his copper-brown shoulders. Mock armour was in right now, but she got the feeling the overlapping metal snake-scales of his tunic weren't designed just for appearances.

'Can't do that,' he said, as if she'd asked him to overlook some minor offence, just this once. 'Always do what I'm told. That's the deal.'

'Yeah, you're well known for your honesty.' Jude slid one hand casually across the hip of her coat. Just a few more inches to the seam of the outside pocket and the pressure point to activate the shock net. 'You should consider breaking the rules once in a while. Keep your adversaries on their toes –'

His vast hand closed on her elbow, forcing her arm flat against her side, into full contact with the hidden steel mesh, just as she hit the pressure point. Five thousand volts arced through the net and earthed, mainly through her. She felt the muscles of her throat contract into a yell that never happened. Then she was face down on the tiles, whining faintly, dim red pulses strobing behind her eyelids.

MultiLegion, who must have taken a considerable amount of the discharge, looked down at her in some puzzlement, unable to work out what had just happened.

'I think,' he said, 'I'm doing just fine so far.'

Sure you are, big guy. But then, I figure you weren't exactly like the rest of us even before someone paid for you to go into a clinic and come out part-Superman and part-God-knows-what . . .

Long muscular fingers bit into Jude's shoulders, tearing the velvet as they dragged her upright. She felt the warmth of his stale, amphetamine-soured breath against the back of her neck. 'Let's go outside.'

The freshening room had emptied in record time, leaving an array of abandoned lipstick, powder and assorted stimulants. It looked like the aftermath of a police raid, waiting for the photographer.

Maybe one of the evacuees would have the consideration to hit an alarm button on the way out. And maybe not. Fitch must have heard something, at some point, or she wouldn't have made it out to the alley in time to see –

But Jude was here to change her past, not relive it, and she couldn't rely on things happening that way again. Maybe she needed them not to. Maybe being half-dismembered by MultiLegion was the price she needed to pay to swing her future away from that present-time suicide drop.

As the giant's hand fell upon her shoulder, turning her towards the exit, Jude found herself praying fervently that it wasn't.

It was only twenty metres from the freshening room to the exit. Twenty metres of people, squeezed body to body by the slow serpentine currents of the crowd, disguising furtive caresses as accidental collisions of hand and body, relishing the excuse to press closer.

No way even to crawl through their legs, or duck under the tables – wrought iron, too heavy for the average brawler to throw around, but Jude had a feeling that MultiLegion wouldn't have too much trouble with them.

Miyahara was still at his table, but he was too busy flirting with a couple of heavily made up Filipinos, fluttering those yard long eyelashes, and there was no way to attract his attention without MultiLegion noticing.

She was trapped. In deference to the assassin's sheer size, the crowd was parting before them; but it was a token movement, a couple of inches at most, and she knew there was nowhere to go.

For a moment, the nodding heads and animated hands dipped out of sight, and she caught a glimpse of Fitch; using some hidden foothold under the bar to pull herself up and snatch a banknote from some drunk who'd obviously been taunting her diminutive stature. Being Fitch, she clawed him across the face before dropping back out of sight again.

Looked like her best hope of rescue was a short, skinny barmaid with a nice smile. Oh, and cartilage enhanced nails, sharp as razors. Jude had been on the receiving end of those once, and removing the scars had been expensive.

Come on, Fitch. Stop hiding tips down the front of your dress, or exchanging bad jokes with the punters in five different languages. Stop doing your job, sweetheart, and look this way . . .

MultiLegion's hand tightened on her shoulder, and they were at the door, trying to ease out unnoticed as a gaggle of tourists wearing Afro-Rap-star bodies pressed crumpled bills into the doorman's hand.

This was her last chance.

A squabble somewhere behind them sent a shock wave through the crowd; the tourists hesitated and stumbled against one another in the doorway, and an elbow caught Jude in the ribs, pushing her against the doorframe.

Her fingers closed on the twin layers of metal, found the crack between them, touched the sensor strip for the main alarm. Then another impact shoved her out into the night, and she stumbled, off-balance, down the steps and into the street.

Well, that explained how Fitch found out.

Club Andro was in East Cross, one of the quieter districts. Trendy, of course: on Millennium Avenue, three streets away, where the ground fell away from under you and teenagers committed rollerblade suicide freewheeling downhill towards the Artists' Quarter, there was something resembling overcrowding. Which, these days, meant that more than one floor in any building was occupied.

But East Cross had never recovered from the Migration; its residents had been wealthy and left en masse, and looters had wrecked most of the buildings even before fire swept in from the abandoned suburbs. The rest of the block consisted of forlorn piles of bricks, softened by patches of buddleia and emaciated gorse. Even the hastily whitewashed walls of the Club, seen in daylight, revealed an undercoat of soot and heat-bubbled paint.

Of course, none of the would-be clubbers queuing at the door for a credit check had ever seen the place in daylight. Nor had the huddle of teenagers who'd been refused admittance, and now loitered across the street, blowing on their cupped hands and scowling hostility at the flickering neon facade. They knew better than to look at their dreams under so harsh a light.

Jude didn't bother to look surprised as MultiLegion steered her into the adjacent alley, a jumble of firebombed recycling bins, broken glass and long-lost underwear. She had a reputation for being undemonstrative, even unemotional. In fact, like most ReTracers, she made a point of hiding her initial reaction to any situation; it made life easier if she had to come back to it at any point.

In fact, just like the first time, she was practically shitting herself.

Harchak was waiting in the shadows at the end of the alley, exactly the way he had before.

She found herself comparing details, looking for the things that had changed, the clues to which way to push the situation. The broken bottles arrayed along the top of the low wall, catching the moonlight like lanterns; the way the ivy had punched through the crumbling brick, curling lustfully towards the dim reflected neon. A drainage channel crossing the alley – she'd stumbled there the last time, had to be careful not to do that again – and there was the fragment of red satin, probably a suspender belt, tattered by crows looking to line their nests in style.

And something else.

The way MultiLegion shambled along behind her, the snuffling of his breath, the way his fingers on her shoulder had seemed more like claws. Okay, he'd never exactly been Mr Civilised – not exactly a prerequisite for the job – but now . . .

The boy, quite obviously, ain't right.

Her heel skidded down the shallow incline of the drainage channel and, startled by her inability to prevent the obvious, she let herself fall. MultiLegion snatched at the small of her back, tearing the coat still further, but she was already on the ground, blinking up at Harchak's luminous grin, rainwater seeping through the knees of her slacks.

'That's where I like them,' Harchak smiled, stopping his blade absently across the silicised surface of his jacket. 'On their knees.'

'Yeah, fuck you too –'

Something was breathing on her cheek.

Turning her head, slow and unthreatening, Jude found herself staring into the wet, red maw of something neither animal nor man.

The eyes were human, blue and clear and infinitely sad, but the head was long, lupine, the skin grey and peeling around enlarged nostrils. It stank of piss and amphetamines and acrid, human sweat.

She turned – on one knee, grinding her best slacks into the mud – and saw the same animal glint in MultiLegion's eyes. The same eyes, the same smell. Variations on the same species.

Miyahara was right. The clinics had gone insane –

And this was definitely not how things happened before.

'Say hello to the nice lady, Fenris.'

White teeth glistened in an ironic smile.

It was a wolf, or it had been once. New, strange things were woven into it now; intelligence and obedience and the cold, clear self-interest that formed the foundations of human cruelty. She wondered briefly, madly, what was going on inside that head, now crammed with artificial understanding of a world it could never actually share.

'You kill me,' Jude rasped, unable to tear her gaze from those cold, tragic eyes, 'and GenoBond will hang you out to dry.'

'Credit me with some intelligence, Jude.' Harchak offered her a hand up. 'If I wanted you dead, I wouldn't have you extracted from the finest rumour-mill in Europe, in front of hundreds of witnesses. I just want a little chat, that's all.'

Spreading her hands in acquiescence, Jude backed off a step.

MultiLegion three paces behind her, the man-wolf to her right, Harchak in front. The wall of Club Andro at her left shoulder, pulsing with transsexual anarchy; to her right, the glass-topped boundary wall, and a wilderness of collapsed cellars, open sewers and twisted pillars of metal and rust.

The skies were empty and a police helicopter wouldn't set down in East Cross anyway. Not just for a backstreet squabble. The best she could hope for from them would be a gas grenade to break up the fight. She was on her own.

The man-wolf hissed softly and began nuzzling the pocket of her coat.

Harchak raised an eyebrow. 'You didn't leave her armed, did you?'

'Shock-net's only good for one charge,' MultiLegion observed, 'and she done that. Got some trank darts, that's all.' A wicked soprano giggle, close and vicious. 'She go for them, Fenris bite her hand off.'

'That seems reasonable.'

Jude wrung water from the hem of her coat. 'That depends on how you look at it,' she muttered.

'I confess to being a little surprised.' Harchak rubbed his

gloved hands together, apparently more from habit than the cold. 'Aren't you ReTracers supposed to hop back in time and extricate yourselves from any dangerous situation before it even happens?'

'That's the idea.'

'So, why are you still here?'

'It's not that simple. I have to know what to undo.'

'You could simply not come to Club Andro tonight.'

Jude shook her head. 'Then you'd come to my place, or catch me another night. No point in delaying things. I need to solve this problem, not avoid it.'

Harchak smiled. 'My thoughts exactly.'

In the blue neon reflected from the rooftop sign, he looked tired and old. He'd been a petty vicelord since Jude was a child, a name warily admired by teenagers all over Little East Bankside. His heart had never been in it, though. He'd been a scientist, once, back when that still had some meaning. There'd been a big house and a good pension and invitations to all the right places.

Then things went wrong. People talked about grudges, official disapproval, enemies in high places. Or maybe it was drugs, or a woman, or prison; no one knew, or really cared. It was the fall that mattered.

Suddenly, he was just a hood in a shabby suit, running unlicensed gene clinics south of the river. The Migration had thrown the city entirely into the hands of his kind and there'd been all-out gang war for years, driving out yet more of the civilian population.

Harchak had survived, but he hadn't prospered. Rumour said he had a few blocks of Victoria Bridge East now, old skinhead territory. She'd heard some stuff about new regening techniques, cornering the marketing in this and that, but everyone in the business claimed they were one step away from the next big thing, didn't they?

What all that had to do with Fenris here, or ReTracers, was entirely another matter.

'Come on, then, let's hear it. I'm missing the entertainment.'

Harchak drew a breath, wincing in the cold, and said, 'I find myself in need of a friend inside the hallowed halls of GenoBond.'

'A spy.'

'Such a harsh word. I was thinking more – someone with her ear to the ground. Her finger on the pulse of government policy. Someone who could pass on anything of interest to a man in my position.'

The wind was biting through her damp clothes, chilling her to the core. She folded her arms around herself, shivering to reinforce the point. It didn't take much acting ability. Fenris growled, but didn't move.

The spare battery connection for the shock-net was under the left arm and it only took an authorised fingerprint to connect it.

'Look.' Keeping her tone low, cooperative. 'I'm not saying this can't be arranged.'

'Good. That would be a very unwise thing to say.'

'But if GenoBond ever trace any leaks back to me, I'll spend the rest of my brief and agonising life strapped to a bench in Internal Investigations, being – investigated internally. And yes, I appreciate that you can hurt me as much as they can. But where does that get you? You want a mole who's not going to get caught. I want to keep you happy, and GenoBond happy, and stay alive. Make sense?'

Harchak nodded.

'So. What kind of information do you want?'

A siren wailed, somewhere out in the night, and the man-wolf snarled. Harchak patted its head to quiet it and it shifted closer to him, resting its head against his leg.

That left Jude a clear leap at the boundary wall. If she was prepared to thrash around in the overgrown, ice-bound bombsite beyond, fighting off a four-hundred-pound assassin, a sentient wolf-thing, and whoever else Harchak had stationed out there to ensure they weren't disturbed.

'I've been hearing rumours,' Harchak admitted. 'That people in high places have taken a dislike to bioteching. People changing identity every five minutes, messing up the paperwork. No way to tell who or what you're sleeping with. No way to be sure if the police officer or the judge is who they appear to be, or some underworld crony in a duplicated body.'

'Hardly a new problem. Anyway, there are always ways to tell. What's this got to do –?'

'I heard they're planning to send a ReTracer back to Year Zero, to stop bioteching techniques from ever being discovered.'

Jude went cold with shock. Just for an instant, the quick fierce revulsion of seeing her world crumble about her. And then it hit her, and she almost laughed in relief.

'That's a pile of shite, Harchak. A conspiracy theory to get the underworld scared. A ReTracer can only travel back through their own past, to a time and place they've been earlier in their life. And there were no ReTracers before Year Zero – because we were created out of a genetic anomaly in one of the earliest clinics. By definition, none of us were alive – even in the womb – before the first clinics opened.'

The lights of a passing taxi-bus glittered in Harchak's black eyes. For the first time, Jude saw the remains of real intelligence there, and wondered if she was out of her depth.

'Can you honestly assure me,' he murmured, 'that Geno-Bond aren't trying to train ReTracers to go back beyond their own lifespan?'

'Of course they're experimenting. Going back further into

the past, or places they've never been. I don't see how it can work – we travel back into our own bodies, and if our bodies aren't there, where will we end up? – but of course they're trying. They're scientists. That's what scientists do.'

'They try. And sometimes they succeed.'

Somewhere down in the Artist's Quarter, where people still had a modicum of civil pride, the newly restored city clock struck one.

Fitch.

On the very stroke of one, just like before. A shadow on the fire escape overhead, a sharp intake of breath, the flash of a gas spray. Harchak staggered, clutching at his face. Stun rounds raked the wall as MultiLegion exploded into action, but Fitch was already gone, dropping into the shadows behind the club. Light reflected from the blades implanted across the back of her hand as she jumped, a glitter of silver falling into the abyss.

MultiLegion, she was ready for. But from up there, Fitch couldn't have seen the creature crouched at Harchak's feet – the creature that hadn't even been here last time, the creature whose teeth were appearing, slow-motion, in a hungry snarl –

Jude must have screamed her name. She was halfway through screaming something, certainly, when the back of MultiLegion's hand caught her across the cheekbone, a casual slap that sent her sprawling. As she clutched for a handhold, her fingers raked fur, and something warm and squirming broke her fall. She gave it the full charge of the shock-net and it screamed like a child.

As she jackknifed, panic-stricken, off the man-wolf's body and back into the shadows, she heard the slow hiss of its final breath, a sound of profound relief.

A snap of elastic as MultiLegion settled infra-red goggles over his face, and he was gone. Into the rear alley, where Fitch had taken shelter. No way back up to the roof, and no way out.

Blinking away the bright flashes of a fledgling concussion, Jude made it to her feet and slithered across the wet stones to Harchak.

The old man was kneeling in a puddle, moaning; hands clenched into fists as he fought the impulse to rub his eyes and drive the irritant further in. He whimpered as Jude ripped open his coat and started going through his pockets, but made no attempt to resist.

There was a knife in the inside breast pocket, tangled among a wad of mixed currencies. Extracting it, she released a shower of notes into the alley, filling the water with what rapidly became paper pulp.

She pressed the flat of the blade against the side of Harchak's neck, just under the chin, where she could open an artery with a flick of the wrist. 'Call him off.'

Harchak coughed like a dying man.

'Call him off and we'll make a deal.'

A sigh of exasperation; then, sharp and clear despite the gas, 'MultiLegion! You're recalled. Take Fenris back to the car and wait for me.'

Silence. Jude pressed the blade in a little harder.

'Now!'

Shambling out of the alley, stun-cannon dangling from one hand, MultiLegion glanced indifferently at them, and turned to obey.

'Fenris,' he observed, pausing beside the body, 'is dead.'

'I know.' Harchak glared at Jude as if she'd murdered some innocent puppy. 'Brittle bones. Must take another look at the sequencing . . . Just take his body back to the car and wait for me.'

Crouching, MultiLegion slung the carcass over one shoulder. His eyes glittered; with anger or tears. As he straightened up, Jude thought she heard him whisper, 'Poor doggie.'

'Poor doggie, my arse.' For someone who'd been chased

up and down an alley by a four-hundred-pound psychopath with a stun cannon, Fitch looked pretty good. She'd changed out of the skimpy bar uniform into a plain red stretch dress, and her hair was brushed back and lightly curled. One shoe was still in her hand, stiletto heel poised for use as a weapon, and the other was missing; her bare legs were splashed with mud and she'd lost an earring. Somehow, it all just added to the charm.

'Nice work, Fitch.'

'You think?' She frowned at the now useless shoe, shrugged, and tossed it over the wall. 'You owe me one fucking big explanation, my love.'

'What a pleasant young lady,' Harchak murmured, trying to shift sideways, out of the puddle.

Jude stepped back, careful to keep her weight evenly balanced, the knife poised to meet any attack. 'Yeah, Club Andro just can't get the staff these days.'

Fitch swore liberally in Korean, but her hand closed lightly on Jude's shoulder anyway.

Feeling Fitch's eagerness to shelter her, protect her, Jude wondered how she'd missed it last time.

But their future fallings-out were the least of her problems right now.

Harchak had made it to his feet, hands raised in surrender. With the club's shimmering neon behind his captors, he was having difficulty focusing on them. 'So? What happens to me?'

'I don't want to fight you, Harchak. I'm letting you go – no punishment, no ransom, and I don't expect any more trouble from you. Deal?'

The old man shook his head in disgust. 'That's the trouble with you government types. No ambition. Let alone greed.'

'I haven't finished yet.'

Harchak turned his watery stare upon her, surprised and impressed.

This had to be it. The way to change her present. To stop Harchak sending another team after her – it had to be him that had got her thrown out of that window, why else would she be here? And all she needed to do to change that was to say –

'I'll take your offer. If I ever get any information on the subject you mentioned, I'll pass it on to you. Pay what you think it's worth. I doubt I ever will hear anything, but . . .'

'Deal.'

And as simply as that, bang, the problem is solved. The vendetta wiped from the record, Harchak's mad curiosity satisfied, my plunge from a skyscraper just another byway in my cluttered memory, another false turning that I reversed back down and then obliterated.

I love my job.

'All right, go. Before we all catch pneumonia.'

Fitch slipped an arm around her waist as she watched Harchak stumble off down the alley; and despite everything she knew now and hadn't then, Jude couldn't find it in her heart to object.

Room Eight was one of the club's socialisation rooms – illegal in a building without an Authorised Bordello licence, and consequently, cleverly disguised as a storeroom by three crates of empty gin bottles placed in the corner.

Quite how the management explained the necessity for a four-poster bed, bath and shower complex, and a holographic open fire projection with genuine zebra skin rug in every 'storeroom' had always eluded her.

Fitch brought a pot of coffee up from the bar, and a bottle with a couple of shots of brandy left in it, and Jude wrapped herself in the quilt and watched her clothes steam dry on the radiator.

'Good thing you came along,' she conceded, playing along

with the echoes inside her head, following the lines of remembered conversation, letting the past repeat itself. 'I wasn't getting along too well alone.'

Fitch smiled and Jude had to smile too, watching the fake firelight play across her face, revealing a tenderness she tried unsuccessfully to hide.

'So,' she said, 'what was all that about anyway?'

'Harchak had heard something . . .' Jude shivered at the memory. 'Some lunatic Club Andro rumour about ReTracer research. Wanted me to feed him information on it.'

'And if Warner and all your GenoBond buddies find out?'

'If this is true, then they're the least of my worries.' She gulped at the coffee, relishing its bitter sting. 'It's not true. It's technophobia, silly skiffy-TV paranoia. So it doesn't matter, because I won't ever have to do it.'

Fitch threw herself onto the bed, settled herself with her back to one vast oak post, her face shadowed by the brocade curtains. Jude watched her blow on her coffee, sip it, grimace. Trying to reconcile the comforting familiarity of her every movement with the bitter revelations of their last encounter. Trying to see Fitch as she used to, before she knew.

'Jude?'

'Mmmmm?'

'Nothing. You just seem – a long way off.'

'I was just thinking.'

Laying a hand on Jude's bare knee, Fitch took the coffee cup from her and set it aside. 'You shouldn't think, you know. It's bad for you. Scientists have proved it. Especially when there are so many better things to do with your time . . .'

She could stay here for ever. The fire, the bed, the brandy. Fitch. If there was a way to freeze time, to live forever in a single moment of joy, Jude would choose this day, this moment.

But there wasn't. And when she returned to her present-past, this moment and all the other moments would still be lost forever.

I hate my job, she thought, and ReTraced.

Forward to her present. She'd fixed it now, surely, she was released –

Air rush, vertigo, terror. She was still falling.

Sick with terror, Jude let herself slide back into the past.

TWO

Geno Bond HQ, three weeks ago

'I really wish you'd reconsider that, Jude,' Warner sighed, settling himself comfortably with his immaculate shoes on the edge of the desk. 'It's a golden opportunity. Moving to the country could be the beginning of a whole new lease of life for you.'

Jude smiled.

Easy one this time.

Welcome to July 2nd. Nice bright summer's day – a rarity now, whatever the Public InfoBroadcasts said about climate stabilisation. She'd arranged to meet Fitch after an early shift at Club Andro; the evenings were long, they'd go down to the Wharf to drink coffee at that crazy Australian's bagel stall and watch the kids testing their handcrafted sailboards, only a hundred apiece, all designs available . . .

Warner was watching her across the desk, fingers pressed together in a gesture that was supposed to indicate deep thought.

'You know I'd go insane in a Hurst, Mr Warner.'

'You've got it all wrong, you know. You're thinking clean living, fresh air and exercise, early to bed. They are human beings, Jude. They do have music and parties – yes, and alcohol and drugs and whatever . . .'

'Yeah, yeah. I'm not stupid enough to believe the newscast image. I just couldn't live anywhere that . . . small. And crowded. Every apartment in every building occupied. It wasn't like that even when I was a kid in the Bankside.'

'No Hurst holds more than five hundred people. Mostly fewer. And think of all that open space, Jude. Grass. Trees. The sea, even. No broken glass and twisted metal, no ugly piles of crumbling concrete.'

Jude grinned. 'That's the other thing. Green is not a natural colour for a landscape. All that vegetation gobbling up the oxygen, it just can't be healthy.'

'I think you'll find that vegetation is a net producer of oxygen.'

'Whatever.'

Warner sighed, admitting defeat. 'Your loss.'

'I think not.' She sat back in her chair, sipping cautiously at her steaming coffee. Espresso, black. Despite the considerable resources at his disposal, Warner never served anything else.

But then, Warner was that type. Straight down the line; nothing added, nothing taken away. Some of the others, the ones who broke the rules but weren't smart enough to hide it, couldn't get on with that. Jude preferred it. You always knew where you were with Warner.

Mostly on the wrong side of the desk, taking the orders and apologising for the unavoidable, but that was life.

His coffee might be fearsome, but he did have the best view in the whole GenoBond building. Panoramic, right across the north of the city. The broken husk of the PO tower foreground, the green smear of one of the parks behind it. Framing the distant greenery, a jagged tumble of roofs and low rise blocks, splattered red and yellow and purple by tarpaulins and folk art. Everything the city had to offer was out there, hidden from the world below: hand-thrown pottery drying on parapets, children's toys abandoned in the sun, a colour-splash of marigolds or potted lavender on a gravel balcony. A face, a voice, a snatch of music from a badly-tuned guitar. A life.

Warner sat with his back to it, blinds half drawn. He'd probably never even noticed.

'And since when have you been so eager to get me out to a Hurst?'

Warner shrugged. Casual as you like, but she wasn't convinced. She'd seen too many casual shrugs from Warner that had turned out to precede suicide missions.

'We consider it prudent to start shifting our resources away from the cities. No rush, things have been pretty stable so far. But once the infrastructure really begins to give way, gang warfare's liable to flare up again, there could be an anti-government backlash . . . Anything might happen. We can't entirely guarantee the safety of anyone remaining in the city, not over the long term.'

'That's not what the Government promised during the Migration, now is it?'

He must have caught her devil's advocate tone, because he smiled, a little. 'We promised that anyone who chose to stay behind was fed and kept safe from full-scale conflicts. But we didn't promise that for their children and their children's children. No promise is open-ended. We're just closing it down a little sooner than people may have expected.'

'You should have gone into politics, Mr Warner. You're wasted here.'

'Oh, politics is far too messy for my liking. I'm more the Phantom of the Opera type. Manipulate from behind the scenes.'

He laughed, to tell anyone who'd bugged the office that he was joking. Jude wasn't sure whether to be convinced or not.

'Now you come to mention it,' she said, after a grimacing swig at the coffee, 'there is a certain physical resemblance.'

'Cheek. I paid a fortune for this one. Famous Arctic explorer. Rugged, dependable and quietly sexy, or so the marketing says.'

Jude shrugged. 'I'm sure I wouldn't know.'

So far, everything was going just the way it had before.

Never mind. Plenty of time. The moment would come, and she'd notice it and act.

'Anyway, the Hursts also need the protection afforded by ReTracers. There have been odd attacks by environmentalists. Banner-waving and sabotage, nothing serious so far – but that's just luck. Sooner or later, the HardGreens will hit something serious.'

'Like a reactor, yeah. And do I want to be on duty at one of those when it blows? I think not.'

Warner laughed. 'Jude. If you were beside the reactor when it blew, you'd skip back and stop it blowing. Net result: it would never have blown in the first place. That's the whole idea, isn't it?'

'Yes, but . . .'

'You are so superstitious.' He sat back in his leather swivel chair, running a hand through his bushy hair as if to show it off. An old gesture, borrowed from the time when keeping your hair into your fifties was your achievement and not a regening clinic's.

'So, what's today's exciting assignment?'

He spared her an exasperated look. He seemed to have this idea that she didn't take her job as a high-level government employee seriously enough. 'VIP minding. There's a Green Urbanites bash in the Park, some festival or other. A couple of German businessmen want to take a look at this quaint ritual, and the Government have decided to ensure that they don't get thrown in the Serpentine or anything.'

This wasn't the job she'd received, first time round.

Not a problem in itself. A lot of things could have changed between living a given day and re-visiting it. Other ReTracers' actions had a knock-on effect, for a start. Rarely enough to change history, but sometimes enough to shift the details of a conversation, change the routine of a working day. And her own changes to the past, at Club Andro, could have had totally random effects upon every day of her life since.

In fact, that was one of the best parts. Living a life that was constantly shifting, where the past was never quite the same twice. Learning to smile when your memories didn't match someone else's, because you'd been there twice, or more, and seen all the different permutations, all the possibilities.

'It should be fun,' Warner was saying. 'Someone of your Luddite leanings should feel right at home.'

'I'm not a Luddite.'

'If you say so. Though I hear some of those SoftGreen girlies are pretty free with their favours . . .'

'Just one problem, Mr Warner. I'm – not operational today.'

Not operational. Polite departmental euphemism for, 'Actually, sir, although I'm forbidden to give you the details, I'm already in mid-ReTrace and the me you're speaking to is from some indeterminate point in the future.'

Outside, a hawk dived into the pigeons on the adjoining roof, triggering an eruption of feathers and shrieking, flapping escapees.

Warner tipped the chair back onto two legs, resting his shoulders against the wall, and looked at her.

Wondering, she could be pretty sure, whether he could risk trying to break the Recommendation.

It would be so easy, wouldn't it? To ask for a stock market tip, a political scandal to sell to NewsTV. To ask if your sick grandmother was going to recover, or just whether you should buy that new suit now or wait for the sale.

They'd catch you, of course. If it took them ten years, or a hundred, somewhere down the line they'd catch you. And someone would ReTrace back to warn a colleague who'd ReTrace back to warn another, until the knowledge caught up with you, backwards through time.

Until one day, about 30 seconds before you would have asked the question, the ReTracer you were about to ask would pull a gun and blow your head off for no apparent reason at all.

'That's fine,' Warner murmured, studying Jude's face as if he expected to find some kind of vital clue there. 'I was going to send Schrader with you anyway. Speaks German. He can handle it on his own. Or you can tag along, have some fun. We're not exactly overworked today.'

Leaving her the choice. Because only she would know what she was here for, what she was searching for.

And even then, she'd only know when she found it.

'Yeah.' Jude watched the sun break through a smear of cloud above the shattered roof of St Pancras. 'You know, I might just do that.'

The Park was a single heaving mass of people.

The official car dropped them across the road, where they were slightly less likely to attract attention – or the traditional bombardment of mud and rotten vegetables for squandering resources and polluting the atmosphere with a private vehicle – and they crossed the empty road to the Alexandra gate in silence.

The two Germans, Hinke and Beck, hadn't actually spoken since Warner introduced them in the GenoBond car park, twenty minutes ago. On his advice, they'd removed their suit jackets and grudgingly replaced them with shabby PlasMacs to hide exactly how expensive their hand-stitched silk shirts were. They didn't look happy about it.

Considering that this was supposed to be their idea of fun, they didn't look happy at all.

Jude looked sideways at Schrader. With his brutally cropped blond hair, a grey shirt buttoned to the neck, and that permanent scowl, he could quite easily pass as a third member of the negotiation team.

Which left her, in a KENSAL PUNK BOYS T-shirt and old jeans, looking like a hanger-on, a streetbird, or simply a complete idiot.

'This is ridiculous,' Schrader muttered. For the first time in a dozen or so glancing, ill-tempered encounters, Jude thought he looked nervous. 'The entire city must be here.'

The fence had been turned into a billboard, hung with damp cardboard signs advertising everything from lab-grown piata crystals (Instant Improvement In Karma Is Guaranteed) to certified organic cannabis. In the few gaps between signs and posters, someone had woven stems of lilac, drooping now in the mid-morning sun.

Inside, every inch of ground between the gate and the Serpentine had been seized by an invading army of stall-holders, streetcorner preachers, hawkers, ladybirds, mollys, and every other variety of the great urban unwashed. It sounded like a riot and looked like an explosion in a colour-blind designer's clothing shop. Jude found herself suddenly terribly sure she didn't want to go anywhere near it.

But she was still walking, propelled by fear of embarrass-ment and the cluster of bodies at her back, and the crowd seemed to be expanding out of the park to meet her in a fog of bad deodorant, ganja smoke and perfume.

At the gates, a woman dressed as a tearful clown pressed a leaflet into her hand. 'Official day of mourning for the planet, come and do your part.'

A sudden surge of escaping children – pickpockets, probably, off to unload their haul – swept them apart. Tiny fingers plucked at her pocket and withdrew, foiled by closures keyed to her fingerprints alone.

Welcome to the Claustrophobia Express, move right down inside the car please, we've plenty more to squeeze aboard.

Hinke, the short one, pushed his spectacles further down his nose and squinted over them at the crowds. 'Your Green Urbanites, I presume.'

'That's right,' Schrader chipped in. Jude got the feeling he was setting things straight now, before she could step in and ruin them for him. 'SoftGreens, the media call them. They advocate anti-technology, back to the land policies, but they're still quite happy to take government food rations and barter vouchers.'

'As are most of your people, it seems.'

'Only those who, for some misguided reason, choose not to participate in the new society we're building in the Hursts.' Schrader smiled thinly at the seething crowds, as if pitying them. 'We continue to provide their basic needs, but we can't justify providing all life's little luxuries here, at enormous cost, when a full and meaningful life is available to them in the Hursts, any time they wish it. If they choose to reject that, well, that's their choice, isn't it?'

Beck and Hinke nodded wisely, exactly on cue.

Jude was thinking of her mother, emerging from yet another benefits office with some browbeaten clerk yelling after her, 'If you won't consider the work available, Ms Di-Mortimer, then you're deliberately removing yourself from the system. Well, if that's your choice . . .'

'C'mon,' she said, forcing herself to head directly for the densest concentration of bodies. 'Let's party. Do you think they sell candy-floss?'

Schrader's furious stare burned into the back of her neck as she walked away.

Lighten up, tight-arse. Compared to the mess I'm trying to sort out, you don't even know what a problem is . . .

She hadn't always been scared of crowds. She hadn't been used to them, growing up in the creeping depopulation of the Bankside, every year another building sliding into disrepair, home to stray cats perpetually locked in single combat with rats half their size. But she hadn't been scared. Not until the day of the Migration.

The shift out to the Hursts had happened quite gradually, for obvious reasons. There simply wasn't enough room on the roads to move sixty-three million people to isolated communities in the middle of nowhere all at once.

But somewhere along the way, the Government decided it needed a landmark, and designated one Saturday as Migration Day. Pushed the system parameters a little, shifted two million on the one day, mostly from the major cities. Carefully chosen people, of course. Smiling, photogenic people in designer clothes, with meek children and cuddly pets.

Confined to the apartment by her mother, who seemed oddly scared by the whole operation, Jude had spent the morning perched in the window seat, watching the chaos.

About a quarter of their block were leaving. She watched them lining up two by two, their bags on the ground between their feet for protection, as the wind raced screwed-up newspaper along the SideRide track and kids hung out of windows to spit ineffectually at them or call them traitors.

Considering all the stuff she'd seen on TV – gardens and rooftop pools and big soft beds with satin pillows – they didn't look that eager to leave. They were young couples, mostly, without children, so she didn't know them. Maybe her mother did, but she didn't seem interested in saying goodbye. Just clattered pans in the kitchen area and scowled at the TV reports as if they were some sort of personal threat to her.

Nobody in the Bankside had a car, of course. The permit alone cost a decade's wages. So the Government sent buses, big green or yellow buses driven by smiling fatherly men with neatly trimmed beards. And while the stupidly grinning couples were loading their patched and polished suitcases, and the cameras played across the crumbling concrete they were leaving behind, the riot started.

A lot of the Bankside residents had just never applied. They liked living somewhere where the police rarely ventured and all the shops still accepted easy-to-steal cash.

But some had filled in the forms and got back cheery letters saying there was no room for them just yet, or they were a little too far down the waiting list, and maybe they'd like to try again next year?

Looking back, she could see why. The Cowleys, whose kids wore police monitoring tags as a proud badge of criminality; the Syals, who ran illegal technology out of the disused Tube station, hawking anti-surveillance and top class encryption to anyone rich and paranoid enough to need it. Their next-door neighbour, Maya Keeley, supporting a tribe of loosely related children by cooking up a new variant on PCP in the shower cubicle. Not at all the kind of citizens the wage-slaves wanted in their brave new world.

It started with squabbles in the bus doorways, raised fists and shouted threats. Her mother had told her to close the curtains, but only in the quiet, automatic way she gave any order she was too tired to enforce. Jude, who knew the rules back to front by that stage, yelled back some garbled assent, and kept watching.

The bus drivers didn't want them on board, not without the right paperwork. The knives came out. The drivers started waving their anti-riot aerosols and pretending they had some idea what to do with them. Then the families and friends and whichever gang they'd been buying protection from barged in, and from there it was downhill all the way.

It wasn't a bad riot, for its time. Twelve dead, couple of hundred injuries. Couple of shiny new buses used for barbecues. The remaining children had wrung a summer's worth of fun playing among the charred bodywork. Too old for spaceship and pirate ships, Jude and her friends had colonised the smallest bus, gossiping and swapping pills stolen from their parents' medicine cabinets.

But on that day, three stories up, nose pressed to the glass, Jude had come to the conclusion that crowds were a bad thing, and it was probably just as well that, with the Migration and all, there weren't going to be any more of them.

Until now.

There were broad paths between the stalls, marked out with painstaking rows of white stones; but they were solid already, people dodging and squirming and sliding round each other. Clumsy, not used to it, and falling against each other by accident and design, trailing arms and legs and clutching hands. It was like Club Andro on the worst night of the year, but without any walls or corners to retreat to.

Schrader grinned down at her as she turned automatically away, and she had to pretend to be admiring the tat on the nearest stall, a scattering of beadwork bracelets and bottles of oils marked DO NOT INGEST.

'Aura crystals,' someone yelled, inches away. 'Guaranteed to see through false exteriors to the soul within. Read the inside, not the false flesh.'

She wondered about buying one and turning it on Warner. What was going on in there, under the jokes and the gentle hints? How come he kept sending her for those testing programs? She'd been twice as often as most people and he still insisted that names just came up at random.

Maybe she should have stayed and grilled Warner for a while. Literally, if necessary. Trap his fingers in his damn espresso machine. He was the key to all this. She must have been on an official mission when the, erm, accident happened. If she could only remember what she'd been doing in that building to get her defenestrated . . .

An elbow hit her in the back and someone coming from the side caught on her jacket, almost spinning her round.

The air was thick with incense from the next stall, she couldn't breathe, she couldn't see, but she had to keep going.

Twenty yards from the first impassable knot of bodies, a failed contra flow between two stalls groaning with brass candlesticks and lamp-stands, Jude lost her nerve completely, and dived through the flapping canopies of the nearest stall into the quiet space behind it.

The grass was churned to mud here, and hours of preparation had trodden layers of evidence into the soil: candy wrappers, used rubbers, scraps of metal and paper and plastic. She imagined an archaeologist digging it up in a thousand years time and trying to decide what kind of arcane religious ritual had been performed here. The honouring of the almost-lost gods Gaia and Mammon, often believed implacable enemies, but getting on very well here, thank you very much.

Even muffled by the stall draperies, the sheer noise of the place shook her. Voices, bells, drums, howling children, sex-noises from the gaudiest tents. She should never have come here, that much was obvious. Maybe she really had made a mistake, corrected the wrong element of today. Maybe she should go back and talk to Warner, or not talk to Warner, or not go into the building –

The possibilities made her head spin.

Or maybe that was just the brazier smoke. Whatever they were burning in there was having a weird effect on the customers. Those two necking over there: well, one of them was dressed as a member of the Order of Chastity, and the other was hardly dressed at all.

And like it or not, she was right in the middle of the festival now. Which meant that whichever route she took out of here, she'd have to walk through a crowd again at some point.

Peering cautiously out between two stalls, Jude caught a

glimpse of the glittering steel curves of the Millennium Bridge, and knew that was her means of escape.

Over the bridge to the other side of the Serpentine – open lawns, just a scattering of escapees who already found the drugs or the trinkets or the partner they'd come to snap up. Then skirt round the mess, and back to the car. She might even walk back to GenoBond. That would give time to cool down. A substantial change of plan, that was what her present-time crisis needed – a whole new approach to the day.

She edged along behind the stalls as far as she could, ignoring the curious stares of traders loitering in the gaps between tables. Mud clogged her heels, slowing her. Parted curtains offered glimpses of the heaving mass of bodies, transformed by distance into one amorphous creature, all flailing limbs and laughing, shouting mouths.

Finally, her channel of safety ran out: blocked by a trio of fortune tellers' booths, all made up in the same threadbare brown velvet.

Time to face her fears.

Sucking air like a drowning woman, Jude pushed her way between stalls, back onto the lank, trampled grass of the official path.

Where Schrader was waiting for her.

'Thought we'd lost you,' he said, in a voice more disappointed than worried.

This seemed to be the quiet end of the festival; mostly thin, earnest-looking men with handfuls of leaflets offering Heaven On Earth Here And Now. They weren't making much of an effort to entrap even the few foolhardy souls drawn down here by the fortune tellers and a noisy machine-weaving display. They just sat there, staring into the crowd, leaflets fanned in their outstretched hands. Waiting for the fish to bite.

'I took the short cut.'

'Hmmm. Right.'

He didn't seem to be making much effort to blend in. No shopping, none of the rusty-pinned badges or printed sashes the campaigners and cultists were handing out. She tried to imagine Sour-face Schrader draped in pink silk declaring 'Save Hunting Hounds' or 'Ban The Combustion Engine', and found her imagination wasn't up to the task.

'What have you done with your Germans?'

'Don't call them that,' Schrader growled.

'So what am I supposed to call them? Italians?'

'Well, "our guests" would do nicely.'

'Guests, Germans, whatever. Where are they?'

Schrader nodded at the two furthest booths. Under the neatly drawn curtains, she could see the turn-ups of their immaculate trousers, already splattered with mud.

'Right. I could have told their fortunes. They'll buy up whatever they came here for, dirt cheap, and go home rich men. Because – any country, any commodity – their sort always do.'

Schrader's scowl deepened. It suited him. He never looked quite right smiling.

'They came here,' he said, 'to research the Hurst system. With a view to emptying their country towns. If that works, the cities follow.'

Them too. Then France, maybe, and Switzerland – they're halfway there already. The Scandinavians next . . .

Until there are no more cities left. Anywhere.

Jude shrugged, aware of how forced the gesture looked. 'That's their business. I'm just here for the local colour, remember?'

'I think not,' the third fortune teller said.

She leant forward into the light: a young woman, her thin face and roughly-cropped auburn hair giving her the appearance of a Victorian street urchin. Deliberate, Jude decided. All calculated to gain sympathy. But hell, it works. It's working on me, anyway. I always did have a soft spot for redheads.

'I don't need my fortune told. I don't believe all that mumbo-jumbo. I make my own fortune.'

'You make your own past, ReTracer. That's all.'

Jude looked to Schrader, to see if he'd said something that had given them away. He just looked uneasy, like he expected the crowd to round on them any second.

'I'm willing,' the redhead said, 'to tell you how to make your own fortune.'

Sighing defeat, Jude fished a coin from her pocket and laid it on the table.

'Let me see your hand.'

Jude extended it slowly. Left hand; always keep your right free for emergencies. The girl's fingers closed around hers, squeezing. Hot fingers, greasy with sweat. Probably on something. Like everyone else within a quarter mile. Beautifully manicured nails, though. A coat of lightly tinted polish, pink, smoothed to a neat curve, so unlike Fitch's –

A shudder ran through her, and she pulled her hand free.

'She loves you,' the redhead said, as if it was obvious. 'Ask yourself: does the difference between you really matter?'

Aware of Schrader right behind her, Jude realised she'd made a terrible mistake. Swallowing, dry-mouthed, she managed, 'Aren't all telepaths supposed to be state registered?'

The girl laughed briefly. 'I'm not a telepath. I can't read your mind. I see what the powers chose for me to see. The powers, and you.'

'All right, fine. I'm not here for a love life consultation –'

Schrader sniggered deliberately, as if he felt it was expected of him.

'Just tell me my future. If you can.'

Turning her hand over, the girl studied her palm for a moment. 'You're an autumn person, Jude.'

Schrader laughed aloud. 'Yeah, orange and brown are so in. But it's going to take a miracle to Colour you Perfect.'

'A passing person,' the girl continued, as if she hadn't heard. 'One who finds beauty in defeat. One who loves the city because it's dying.'

'The city's always been dying,' Jude murmured, unsure what else to say.

'It's time you realised that there's beauty in victory too.'

'I don't plan to fight any wars.'

'Life rarely goes as we plan. You asked for your future; now you have it, accept it.'

Jerking her hand free, Jude snapped, 'Some future. Platitudes and generalisations. You haven't told me anything.'

'Your future lies in your past. You can only go forward by going backwards.'

Which is exactly what I'm doing. ReTracing. Looking for the key act to undo.

Both hands on the table, Jude leant into the booth until their faces almost touched. 'How far?' she whispered. 'How far back do I have to go?'

'The scale starts at zero.'

Year Zero?

'Bullshit,' Jude snarled, and turned away.

'What's the problem, Jude?' Schrader sniggered, tailing along behind her as she shoved her way through the lines of dealers at the foot of the Millennium Bridge. 'Didn't you get your money's worth?'

'Aren't you supposed to be keeping an eye on your bloody VIPs?'

'They can take care of themselves for a moment. It's not like they're stupid. Or American.' A final sprint, and he fell into step beside her. The bridge was busy and most of the crowd flow against them, but people shrank away from them, leaving them plenty of room to pass.

Shrank away from him, Jude corrected. From the man in the suit and the sunglasses and the wage-slave scowl. From the one who takes such delight in dressing different, acting different, proving he doesn't belong.

Why is he following me?

'Jude, wait. Let's talk.'

He actually sounded apologetic, which was a first. The few times she'd shared an assignment with him, he'd spent the whole time throwing his weight around and angling for the credit. Maybe the vibe here was rubbing off.

She slowed, a little.

'Look. Warner told me. That you're not operational. And I thought, well, if there's anything you want to tell me –'

Oh, this is all I need . . .

Jude looked away. At the main expanse of the park, and beyond; at the Serpentine, a few inches of clear water shimmering over a solid crust of mud and heavy metals.

'Schrader, are you trying to break the Recommendation?'

He looked sharply at her – the way someone would if they thought you were mocking them, which puzzled her for a moment. Then he shrugged and said, 'I can change my life any time I feel like it, Jude. I don't need the gory details of your future to do that. I just wondered if I could help, that's all.'

Wonderful. Ice-box Schrader gets overcome with emotion. Just to complete her day.

'The fact is, I've been meaning to talk to you for a long time.' He drew breath, looking so much like a teenager about to proposition some impossible dream date that she almost laughed. 'I've always felt we have a lot in common. Much more than you realise. But let's start with, oh, the same determined outlook on life, the same drive –'

'Schrader, if you're trying to get inside my pants, forget it.'

Utterly unembarrassed, Schrader smiled. 'Get with the technology, Jude. I can always have the same operation your girlfriend had.'

He was a tall man and well built; it took all her strength to swing him round and slam him against the bridge railings. But he wasn't ready and, before he could react, Jude had his wrists pinned against the handrail and was screaming into his face, 'You heap of shit, Schrader, you keep your nose out of my –'

On the banks of the Serpentine, clearly visible through the metalwork, a tragedy was three seconds away from happening.

'– business.'

Three steps from the edge of the river, a woman was running. There were people running after her; two, perhaps three, using the loose and scattered groups of bystanders as cover. Another domestic incident, and there had probably been a dozen far worse already. Any minute now, some stallholder's bodyguard would intervene. Violence had a way of escalating and violence was bad for business. There'd be some shouting, the auburn-haired woman would flounce off in a fury, yelling that it was all a misunderstanding, they'd fade back into the crowd and everyone would go back to buying and selling and stealing –

Only this time, it wasn't going to happen.

Jude could feel it. The way you did sometimes when you went back to a major crisis point; the death of a great leader, the small print of a vital promise, one of those rare and tiny moments that makes or unmakes a world. The way you did when the world split in two and on one side, the future you remembered, *on the other, a future you never imagined possible. A future* as easy and familiar *where everything is new and strange* as your own breathing *a future where this* never happened, where this *terrible* running stranger is a Woman of *Importance* No Importance At All *if only I could* just remember *that*.

Jude blinked.

Worming free from her grasp, Schrader stepped sideways, his face creased with concern. 'What the hell's wrong with you, DiMortimer?'

'There,' she whispered. 'Down there.'

Following her stare, he turned.

Down by the Serpentine, the running woman veered aside from an on-coming couple, turning towards the river. *And in this reality, the grass is dry* And in this? Wet grass, treacherous. *She can catch herself and turn* shoes, who knows the cause, but *and sprint away up the bank* either way –

She slipped.

Too close to the edge, too close to turn, to jump, and too far away for anyone to help her. Off balance, she threw out one hand to break her fall; but there was only the river behind her, and her outstretched arm hit water, then mud, then the solid crust.

The crust cracked beneath her, and she went under. Four feet of waste down, half a century of illegal dumping and blind eyes turned. The SoftGreens had managed to lock it away under a chemical-sustained crust, and a little clean water ran over the top, giving the shallow illusion of normality. But down below . . .

The woman's legs spasmed once and sank, sucked under the heaving, bubbling mud. It was shallow enough for her to stand up and walk back out again. But she wouldn't. One breath, one mouthful, one splash of that . . .

The only way for Jude to escape it was to close her eyes, but that didn't help, just fixed the memory like a photograph in her head.

And when she opened them again, Schrader was staring at her, like he couldn't see what all the fuss was about.

'You have to ReTrace,' Jude blurted, 'and rescue her.'

'For God's sake, keep your voice down!' He glanced up and down the deserted bridge, shaking his head in disbelief. 'A lot of these Luddite fanatics think we're servants of the devil or something. I don't think we should be advertising –'

'Didn't you hear what I just said?'

Schrader turned back towards the river. The water was thick with disturbed silt; people were moving hastily away, clamping handkerchiefs over their faces as curls of sulphurous fumes rose from the deep.

'It's a waste of resources,' he said.

'ReTracing doesn't take any resources!' Jude screamed, oblivious to the stares they were attracting from the rabbit-in-headlights revellers. 'I felt a Split. A big one. That woman was important for some reason. Her death changed things – big things. You know the drill. It's vital that you get back there and save her.'

Schrader stared at her for a moment, as if sizing up his opponent in a forthcoming prize-fight. For the first time, she felt a shiver of apprehension.

'I didn't feel anything,' he said.

'Well, I did.'

'Well,' he whispered, barely audible over the murmur of horror spreading through the crowd below, 'I didn't.'

'What's it going to cost you? Is it really too much just to help a fellow human being?'

His mouth wrinkled in disgust. 'She was a SoftGreen, Jude. A wastrel, spending her life chasing fantasies. Worthless. Who am I to undo the ironies of post-industrial pollution?'

'You heartless bastard.'

Shrugging, Schrader turned back towards the festivities. 'So file a report.'

And he was walking away, back to the Germans and the festival and the utterly irrelevant, leaving her with the bitter aftertaste of failure, and a sudden, new understanding.

He felt it. He knows what happened here. But for some reason, he wanted it to.

Jude pressed her face against the cold metal railings, waiting for the body to surface. It might take a while, and it wouldn't be recognisable when it did, but . . .

Auburn hair.

Just like the woman in the fortune booth.

'Oh shit.'

And she is back in her future-present; and still falling.

This is a tough one. She's never had to make more than three journeys to resolve a single problem before. Four is incredibly rare. Five almost unheard of.

No time.

ReTrace –

THREE

The Bankside, fifteen years ago

'Hey, Drosser!'

A child's challenge, fierce and shrill, slicing the still night like a razor. She blinked. Dark skies overhead, midnight blue horizon hazed with smog. Her fingers were numb, her treasured padded polyfabric jacket blazed blue and red under the faded streetlights. Cold air burned her lungs like acid. Curtains twitched and settled at the high windows surrounding her, satisfied that whatever outrage was in progress was no worse than usual.

'Jude DiMortimer,' the voice demanded, ringing from the closed windows and the icy roofs. 'You gonna shut up your boasting and run the Sidewalk, or not, Drosser?'

Jude lifted her face to the glow of the muddy yellow streetlights, and smiled.

Little East Bankside, still and silent as the grave in a January frost. Weather Control switched off the city's modifier towers a couple of nights a year. Just long enough to drop the temperature a couple of degrees below freezing, covering the city with an icing-sugar frost. It gave them a chance for essential repairs, and the old folks a chance to hold their grandchildren up to the windows and boast, 'When I was a child, it was like this every night.'

The police always made sure they had pressing paperwork to do on a Frost Night; because motorbikes and black ice don't mix and, let's face it, no sane person was going to go out on a night when the air temperature actually fell below freezing.

Sanity was a commodity in very short supply on Little East Bankside.

Mum, of course, thought Jude was tucked up safe in bed; but vital-signs monitors were designed to monitor sickly babies, not kids old enough to find the ALARM SILENCE switch. And now Mum, like parents up and down the city, was dozing in front of the Self-Education For Wealth channel, secure in the proximity of a child who was actually out on the frozen street, screaming dares and throwing paintbombs in an unofficial Night of Misrule.

Jude shivered, tugged the coat zipper right up to her throat, and took a good look around.

She was sitting on the steps of the SideRide terminal, directly opposite her current abode, the vast grey silhouette of Block 24 of the Prescott Social Housing Development.

Squinting up past the pseudo-Victorian streetlamps, she could just make out blue TV flicker at the window of their main room. Mum was still up, then. Better hope she gave up on Self-Education and went to bed before Jude tried sneaking back inside, or there'd be hell to pay.

Block 24 was an Exemplary Residents block: separate living and sleeping quarters, hot water on tap and wall to wall carpet, an unheard-of luxury. But any serious misdemeanor – like the one she was currently considering committing – would get them transferred back to one of the basic blocks in an instant.

The threat stirred faint resentment in her, and a flush of guilt. Mum had worked hard to get them classified Exemplary Residents, and Jude didn't want to go back to a bare concrete room any more than she did.

Standing up, she pushed the thought aside. Just one answer to that, kiddo. Don't get caught.

She checked the street, registering flickers of movement in the alleys or along the glazed-in fire escapes. Adults came out to play on Frost Night, too. Dangerous games involving knives and strangling cords, thefts, contracts and old scores.

No danger to her, though. Bankside kids knew better than to get involved; Bankside adults knew better than to tangle with cocky streetwise brats who could scream like divas and knew every short cut and escape route for twenty blocks around.

No police. No movement from the automatic cameras that were supposed to monitor the street 'for your security'. They hadn't worked in years. No 'copter lights visible between here and the neon-hazed horizon.

It was looking promising.

Sitting right here, she was safe anyway. The steps of the SideRide were neutral territory. If some suicidally dedicated police officer did happen along, Jude could say she'd just disembarked. Slipped on the ice, maybe, and sat down to rest her ankle before limping home. No danger there.

The danger lay in accepting Lazy Jay's challenge.

Lazy Jay, currently leaning out of a third floor window in Block 23, watching the night's events with open disdain.

He was nine, a whole year older than Jude; a scrawny Nigerian boy descended from some long-overthrown tyrant, raised penniless, bitter and utterly convinced of his natural superiority to the ragamuffins of the Bankside. He'd thrashed most of the other aspiring bullies and gang leaders in the Prescott into submission years ago, and established himself as leader of the most unruly and admired pre-teen gang, the Electric Volunteers. Even Jude, who thought him an arrogant racist poseur, had to admire his determination.

'Well, Jude?'

He was wearing a coat – fake fur, fashionable, if a little camp – but he wasn't coming out to play. In a flash of premonition, his parents had a disabling switch installed in the prosthesis that reinforced his withered leg, and when it was off, he couldn't do much more than hobble around clinging to the furniture.

Jude looked up at him; a tall, taut silhouette against the thin pink light of the standard bedroom fittings. 'Wassa matter, Lazy Jay? Lost your crutches?'

Even from the other side of the street, she heard him snarl in fury.

Dangerous game she was playing. They'd had a scuffle or two already, the usual schoolyard disagreements. Jay was good with his fists, but Jude was faster on her feet, and her mother's last boyfriend had taught her some unorthodox kick-boxing manoeuvres. By the time the school guard had waded in, the fight had become a stand-off, and an uneasy truce has ensued.

Until tonight.

The rest of the Electric Volunteers had wandered off several minutes ago, bored by the familiar ritual of insults and challenges. They'd gone a few stops down the SideRide, but the sound of it, looking for someone else to harass. She could hear their yells as they competed in some kind of antisocial behaviour; probably jumping high enough to hang off the ceiling girders and hit the EMERGENCY STOP button.

She was alone with Lazy Jay and the night.

'You still stood there, DiMortimer? What's wrong, you forgot your mace?'

God, she'd forgotten that. Her mother forcing her to take a mace spray to school – the new sort, where they took a blood sample and then engineered your spray so it worked on everyone except you. The Volunteers had thought that was howlingly funny. Mummy's little girl can't take care of herself without a mace spray.

Well, they'd thought it was funny until Kohl grabbed it,

tried to spray her with it, and only succeeded in getting hospitalised by breathing in the splashback while Jude, right as rain, laughed her head off.

Oh yeah. Best days of your life, for sure.

'You should sort your parents out, Jay,' she yelled. 'The clinics can fix legs now. Legs, arms, faces . . . Hey, you could have the complete overhaul. You certainly need it.'

'Pity they can't fix brains, Drosser. We'd book you in double speed.'

Jude grinned. 'I can't afford it. But you, you've got the ancestral millions at your disposal. Creamed off – no, I mean gratefully donated by the old country, isn't that right?'

The ancestral millions had ended up in the pockets of the faithful retainer who'd been smuggling them out of the country, and none of the family liked to be reminded of it. Particularly not the one who needed it most.

A flash of white teeth, the glitter of narrowed eyes. 'Don't jeer me, Drosser. You said you was gonna Sidewalk. Gotta big mouth, kid. Got the balls to go with it?'

'Got more'n you have, cripple boy!' She was on her feet now, screaming, consumed by the childish fury that springs from inner fear. 'I'll show you. You wanna display, I'll give you a display.'

And she was down the steps and heading along the pavement.

Little East Bankside had been quick to take the anti-pollution laws to heart. No more private cars meant no more drive-by shootings, no more kerb crawlers, no more mass ram raids. And those deserted roads would make a perfect track for the Mass Person Conveyors the Euro-Fund had just authorised.

FORGET THE SIDEWALK, the strangely Americanised adverts had screamed; TAKE THE SIDERIDE. Simple, easy to police, and totally pollution free.

The fact that people might not want to travel everywhere on a endless loop of slow-motion conveyor belt didn't seem to have occurred to anyone.

There were improvements. They glassed in the tracks, protecting travellers against wind and weather. Allowed entrepreneurs to fill a section with seats and rent them out, even set up refreshment areas or grocery stalls. After all, the journey out to the Municipal Quarter, home of most of the menial jobs that Bankside residents were best qualified for, could take up to two hours.

Strangely enough, no one seemed too impressed.

Then, in a flash of divine inspiration, a minor council functionary hit upon the perfect solution. Simply place an official entrance/exit every hundred yards – and make it illegal to travel more than 125 yards on foot.

Pavements were solely for getting you from your front door to the nearest entrance/exit and back. Anyone found actually walking down them was obviously up to no good, and once the Bankside police pulled you in, they always found some charge or other that would stick. Their productivity bonuses depended on it.

But on Frost Nights, there wasn't a police officer in sight.

In theory.

She was drawing close to the next entrance point: a couple of concrete steps down from the raised conveyor belt, a simple archway in the glass shelter. One hundred yards, entrance to entrance. About forty paces beyond that, she'd be breaking the law.

Driving her frozen hands deep into her pockets, Jude drew a long, tremulous breath.

She remembered this night very well. Remembered going eight paces beyond the entrance point, then ten. And hesitating. Thinking about the cameras staring down from the lampposts. Her mother's proud grin as they accepted the lease on the apartment in Block 24. The empty grey box that had been their last home.

Another step. And another –

And then, she'd turned and fled. Running like a maniac, ignoring Lazy Jay's screams of triumph and promised retribution; bolting up the stairwell and fumbling the entry code at the apartment door, tiptoeing past her mother, asleep in the chair, to hurl herself into bed and sob shamefully into her pillow.

The next day, four of the Electric Volunteers had caught her alone in a school corridor and broken her nose with a monkey-wrench. And that was only the beginning.

She didn't know what all this had to do with her present time dilemma, but it was pretty obvious what she'd come back here to do.

Shadows danced in the arc of light cast by the SideRide entrance, startling her. But it was only the Volunteers. She recognised Kohl, the dumpy Austrian boy with the full, feminine mouth and a rumoured fascination with women's underwear. And Kali Peitrino, shipped off to Juvenile Detention last year for an almost fatal cyanide-bomb attack during Advanced Chemistry. She'd been back in the Bankside for a few weeks now, thought not in school. Run away from Juvie, probably. People said the guards turned a blind eye to escape attempts, if it was someone they'd be glad to see the back of, and she could well imagine that applying to Peitrino.

They, and the younger, shyer members hovering at their backs, were just here to watch tonight. Ranged on the outer steps, muffled up, blocky and unreal against the light.

'Where you going, Jude?'

Drawing level with the entrance, Jude paused to try out that raffish curl of the lip she'd copied from some monochrome movie star last weekend.

Only ancient films were available on Free-TV, real museum pieces with fuzzy soundtracks and edit marks. She resented that for a long time. But eventually, she'd grown to like the sharp, shadowy black and white Daily Classics – and even the evening diet of tearjerkers and transparently obvious murder mysteries. They gave her a whole new repertoire of heroes, an endless private world of quotes and allusions and knowing smiles that none of the other children could understand.

They gave her a window on the past, and, though no one at school seemed to understand, she knew that was important for some reason.

'Gonna phone your mam, Drosser. Tell her you're outside, playing bad games.'

'Phone your own while you're at it,' Jude responded. 'Maybe they'll let her out of prison to come fetch you.'

Peitrino spat at her, though she was too far off to make much of a target, and began rattling something metallic in her pocket.

There didn't seem to be any point hanging around.

Ignoring the hoots and yells of derision from the Volunteers, Jude strolled off down the pavement.

It was familiar enough territory. She knew kids in Blocks 22 and 21, though she'd normally have obviously taken the SideRide to visit them. The police were always around, and seizing an eight-year-old for sidewalk violations was an easy way for them to get back to the station and waste an afternoon on the paperwork, indoors, where they were slightly less likely to get shot at.

In the bleached starlight, the mock-stone edifices of Block 22 took on a disturbingly Gothic air. Huddled pigeons, or illegal windowboxes decimated by acid rain, served as gargoyles, and the blue shimmer of unseen TV screens animated the interiors of the rooms, creating strobing patterns of movement and shadow.

There was movement on the other side of the street, and noise. She slowed; but, even through the grubby glass of the SideRide tunnel, she could see what the couple in the alley were up to, and they were having far too much fun to worry about a traffic violation.

Squeezed between child-curiosity and adult-prurience, Jude found herself blushing.

By the time she passed the imposing front doors of Block 22, the jeering Volunteers had fallen silent.

She'd broken the law by now, covered more than 125 yards, but there was no one around to bother her, and she wanted to leave no room for doubt or denial. If she walked to the next entrance, two stops from her starting place, she'd have covered an indisputable 200 yards, and she could ride back home in triumph, past the chastened gang members.

She should issue a challenge of her own as she passed. Get something in before they had a chance to belittle her achievements, turn the tables –

Fingers closed around Jude's upper arm. Her feet went out from under her as hands clawed her into a recessed doorway.

She fought upright, kicking out against shadows, consumed by panic. Adult-self thinking: face it, stray pre-pubescents got raped to death in alleys without the residents batting a eyelid even on ordinary nights, and out alone on Frost Night she was just asking for it, didn't have a chance –

As a hand tried to clamp an inhaler mask on her face, she pushed sideways in the suffocating grip. It loosened, very slightly. Not enough to get free, but this was only stage one. Panic overcoming all thoughts of dental hygiene, she leant forward and bit down hard on the thin, ulcerated wrist.

The skin broke. Someone screamed like a kicked cat and, gagging, Jude wormed free and ran for her life.

The mask clattered out onto the pavement in front of her,

and she had the presence of mind to kick it away, into the decorative border of litter edging the SideRide track. Black market clinics would fill those with anything you asked for: sedatives, muscle relaxants, will suppressants, whatever fell off the back of a military truck this week.

She didn't stop to look back until she reached the steps of the next SideRide entrance.

The doorway was empty.

Breathing hard, Jude trudged up the steps to safety.

'Looks to me, young lady,' said the woman on the opposite track, 'like you've had rather a fright.'

Jude looked up at her.

She was about thirty, but since regening had really started to take off, you couldn't rely on that. Smartly dressed, too; silk overcoat and real leather shoes, too smart for the Bankside. Which meant she was police. Or an educational investigator. Maybe a God-squad type, the sort her mother had trained her never to open the door to.

Any of which meant trouble. But she was on the southbound track, exactly where Jude needed to be. No way home without riding along behind her. And Jude didn't really feel like hanging around out here, not any more.

'I'm fine,' she said. Stepping onto the nearer track, the northbound one. Dawdling as she crossed it, so the relative motion of the tracks put some distance between them.

But the moment she stepped aboard, some fifteen feet behind her interrogator, the woman turned, weight poised on one foot like a model, and asked indulgently, 'Of course, your mother knows you're out?'

'Been to see my dad.' Pulling a wry face, she added, 'Access visit.'

That usually shut adults up. She'd discovered early on that they all hated talking about absentee parents, usually with a vehemence in inverse proportion to how many they actually knew.

But Miss Leather Shoes and Matching Handbag wasn't giving up.

'Maybe,' she said, 'I should walk you back to your apartment. Check you get home all right.' She smiled, as if they were about to share a secret. 'I don't have to tell your mother anything if you don't want me to. If you'd rather not scare her. I can just come to the door.'

'Well,' Jude said slowly, as if thinking it through. 'I don't know. There's been a lot of robberies around here recently. I mean, they won't touch me, they can see I've got nothing to steal. But you . . . I think you should stay on the SideRide. The security cameras, you see. They won't try anything as long as you stay on the SideRide.'

Twenty yards to her stop. The SideRide seemed to be slowing down, time stretching to prolong her agonies. She could have walked faster, let alone run. How had she ever put up with this? How had anyone?

The woman smiled and snapped open the clasp of her handbag. One gloved hand dipping in, precise, exact, a movement she'd rehearsed a thousand times. 'Well, you're probably right. But why don't you take my Z gas spray, just in case?'

Jude was watching her hand. Closing around something much bigger than the lipstick-sized spray canister. Drawing it out of the bag, into the light. Metal. An immaculate curve of grey metal –

Jude threw herself face down on the rubber track, and the first round took out the shelter behind her in an apocalyptic shower of glass.

No time to think, no time for adult-self to intervene. Pure instinct was running the show. Pushing hard against the track, Jude rolled backwards. Over the raised edge of the track and off, down the steps of her stop. They weren't quite level yet, and she cracked her ankle against the archway pillar. The impact swung her round, from parallel to head-first, just as the second round punched into the step beside her head. Shredded concrete lacerated her face.

Rolling upright, Jude ran.

No, adult-self was screaming; you're an easy target, running. Get under the track. A child will fit down there. You've done it before. Make her get off and search for you.

Too late. Jude the Older And Wiser could have taken control, changed child-self's mind. That was the whole point of Re-Tracing. But she was already most of the way to Block 24 –

And the woman wasn't shooting at her any more.

Colliding with the outer doors, Jude screamed her entry code and jackknifed flat against the wall, making the most of the limited cover.

No shots, no noise, no following footsteps.

What the hell was happening here?

The code finally verified, the doors clicked open, and Jude hurled herself through, using her weight to force the door closed as fast as possible. Bulletproof glass, the advertisement claimed. Perfect safety in the Prescott development.

Unless you happened to be Jude DiMortimer, obviously.

The street outside was empty.

Her breathing had almost stabilised. Pressing her shaking hands to the cold glass as if that would steady them, Jude scanned the long glass corridor of the SideRide.

The woman had disappeared.

Off the other side and into the alleys, obviously. Who'd rely on the SideRide as a getaway vehicle? Yup, that had to be it, because obviously, people don't just disappear . . .

Over in Block 23, Lazy Jay had closed his bedroom window. He was just standing there now, looking at her like she'd grown horns. She couldn't decide if he was scared, or impressed, or jealous.

She tipped him a cheery salute – her hands didn't shake

as badly as she'd expected, from that distance he probably couldn't tell – and turned away.

At least – all other things being equal – she was going to wake up in a body without a crooked nose.

I wonder what Fitch is going to make of that?

The door to the apartment still creaked.

Of course it did, she told herself, taking the weight with one bruised arm as she slipped through the gap. It creaked until the day they threw us out in preparation for the redevelopment that never happened. Probably still does.

And yet it surprised her still; the familiar two-tone creak, the flicker of the TV, the way her mother's hair fell across her face as she dozed in the armchair, legs drawn up to her chest to protect herself from unseen enemies. Her adult-self ached to rush across the room and curl up in the last remaining inches of chair seat, cradled between her mother's cotton nightdress and the tatty velvet cushions.

But she knew it wouldn't make any difference. Her mother would wake and hustle her off to bed, muttering darkly about clingy children and the terrible fates that awaited them in the world. And even if she didn't, everything would all turn out the same in the end. If there was anything she could ReTrace to that would change that inevitable parting, she hadn't found it yet, and she certainly wouldn't find it here.

Tiptoeing through the ripples of light the TV cast on the grey carpet, she passed behind her mother's chair and into the open bedroom doorway.

The nightlight was still on, glowing green like some alien entity come to haunt her dreams. She'd never liked it, but her mother seemed to think nightlights were somehow necessary, and she'd been too embarrassed to confess her fears.

In the underwater glow, her mother's unmade bed loomed, filling most of the room. She had to climb over it to reach her own – which meant taking off her shoes and replacing them in the right spot on the rack, trying not to drop mud on the carpet. Not that anyone would notice, the state it was currently in.

Clothes off, nightdress on; three or four well-rehearsed movements, the routine of a child who went through this secret ritual almost every night. Then cold sheets and traces of lavender scent on the pillow, squeezing her eyes tight shut as she heard a long yawn from the next room.

It was a game. She hadn't realised that until years later. Her mother, too proud to admit her failure, curled up in that chair every night, waiting to feign sleep so she didn't have to issue scoldings that wouldn't be heeded and orders that Jude would ignore. Keeping the peace, saving face.

As her mother's silhouette loomed in the doorway, Jude opened her eyes and said, 'Do you ever worry about me?'

Her mother tensed visibly, suddenly faced with things she'd kept at the edges of her vision for so long.

'That someone might be out to get me?'

A slow breath, and the silhouette settled on the edge of the larger bed. 'Someone at school, you mean?'

But there was concern in her voice and Jude was in no mood to keep up the child pretence. 'Someone. Anyone. Maybe someone from the government. Someone who knows that I'm different.'

Her mother's fingers touched her mouth, quick and hard, as if she could force the words back in somehow. 'You're not different. We've talked about this –'

Oh yes. I remember those conversations; and the crying myself to sleep afterwards, wondering why she couldn't see the obvious . . .

'And I've told you. They're just memories, fantasies, games you play inside your head. You're not different.'

'Because if I was, everything would change, wouldn't it?'

The silhouette straightened abruptly. 'If you keep this up, things will definitely change, I'll tell you that for nothing. If they find out you tell these ridiculous stories. They'll take you away and give you drugs to sort your head out.'

'They'll take me away because I have an ability that very few children have. Today, tomorrow –'

Don't tell her, you can't change it, you can't take the risk.

'Whenever. It's going to happen.'

Her mother stumbled back a step, fell against the bed, and crumpled onto it, breathing hard. 'Is that what you think? Is that what you want?'

'No.' She meant it, she'd always meant it, but the words came out flat and accusing, and her mother turned away. 'But it's what I get. I'm sorry. But I have to know if there's anyone who knows – and who'd want to kill me because of it.'

There. Cover blown. Better hope this never gets back to Warner . . .

Her mother pressed her hand to her forehead for a moment, as if suddenly afraid her skull was splitting and everything was going to come tumbling out.

'You're doing it now, aren't you?' she said.

'Mum –'

'I told you, you mustn't. You can't keep doing this. They'll find out about you, and then you know what will happen.'

Something tugged at the edges of Jude's consciousness, dragging her unwillingly towards the inevitable future.

'I'm sorry. Mum.'

And the nightlight glow expanded to fill the room, and everything was gone.

Oh God, no.

Still falling.

FOUR

Morphotech Offices, three months ago

And there she was, standing outside the shiny office block, looking up at the garish 'before and after' pictures pasted in the cracked, dirty upper windows, and thinking, It would be so easy.

The sun was shining, though the sky to the west was still streaked with grey, and fledgling rock-pools were forming among the broken paving stones. It was strangely quiet. The rain had driven the respectable citizens of Monopolist's Wharf back to the offices where they'd once worked and now squatted, dreaming of lost grandeur. The less respectable had simply moved on, seeking shelter in the down-market pubs and cafes in adjoining streets. Here, among the glistening and battered skyscrapers, monuments to another, inscrutable age, Jude was all but alone.

Thinking exactly what she'd thought the first time.

I only need to sign the paperwork.

No one can stop you, not after you've signed. Not the police, not Warner, not even you yourself. No going back. I mean, why bother? If you decide you don't like it, it only takes another 48 hours to change back.

Leaning her full weight against the door, an intricate design of steel and glass, Jude eased it open.

They'd done the place up nicely. Knew what their customers wanted. A little class, a little taste of how things used to be down here, before commerce went green and moved out to the Hursts, and greed fell, yet again, out of fashion.

Dim lighting with spotlights picking up carefully placed plants or display boards; the reception desk neatly repaired, the carpets relatively clean. A hand-painted sign over the brass plaque that would have identified the building's original function (and owners): MORPHOTECH INDUSTRIES in big gold letters, solid and reassuring. PURVEYORS OF BIOTECHING SERVICES FOR OVER A DECADE.

The 'classy operation' act was obviously working. They had customers, even in this weather. She'd never been in anywhere upmarket, but she'd gone window shopping with friends in the cheaper, backstreet places, and she knew all the customer types by sight.

The old man and the fidgety woman hovering around the displays nearest to the doors. They'd be the loiterers. Timewasters, in out of the rain. And the kids. A couple of eight-year-old music fans in Prissy Boy T-shirts, far too young to buy, waiting to see if someone would take their eyes off their wallet before security got round to throwing them out.

There'd also be – yes, there in the shadows – a single, scowling figure waiting for the crowds to dissipate so he could enquire about the availability and/or legality of some dubious alteration. This time it was a young dark-haired man with purple eyes. Eyes right out of a jar. He'd probably be accommodated. They almost always were. People tended to overestimate how original and daring their cherished fantasies actually were.

And then, the real customers. Three girls in short skirts arguing over the shape of a mannequin's nose as they shuffled and smirked. An old woman taking a seat in a consulting room, smoothing her red dress with prim and wrinkled hands.

And Jude. Standing at the reception desk, twisting the

strap of her shoulder bag nervously between her fingers, trying to look no more or less nervous than the real customers.

I could walk out of here as anything. Anyone. Warner would probably never even find me.

Is that why I've come back here? Is that what's necessary to stop myself going skydiving without a parachute in a few months time?

But regening can, quite accidentally, damage the genetic accident that gives us our abilities – and if I lose the ability to ReTrace, how will I get back to my present?

Too many questions. Just go with your past and see what happens.

She cleared her throat meaningfully.

The slim, dark-eyed man at the desk looked up with a smile that could have come straight from their catalogue – no. 17, Trustworthy Public Servant. 'Madam. May I be of some assistance?'

Jude shrugged. Muffled in the neatly buttoned wool coat, the pleated skirt, the trappings of respectability, she found that guilty indecision came easily to her. 'I was thinking of making a few alterations.'

'But of course,' the young man said, taking a moment to straighten his ill-fitting jacket as he stood up. 'Would madam care to step into a consultation room to discuss her requirements?'

Same room as before. Old executive office, salvaged furnishings and a desk laden with catalogues. She paused to scan the titles. *Eyes, ears, noses; limbs, upper and lower.* Same gentle slant of light through the dirty glass as she hung her coat on the single hook behind the door, registered how cold it was, and regretted it. The receptionist clearing his throat in that same nervous fashion as he joined her, a slab of paperwork under one arm.

Same, same, same.

Why have I come back here?

This was a routine job. Emma DiFlorian went missing. Everyone worried for a while. Someone saw a woman of a different racial type who looked exactly like her, then lost her in the backstreets of the theatre district. Recent paperwork was pored over. An Emily DiFlorian was found to have checked into Morphotech twelve days previously for a complete re-gening. The catalogue pages and photographs of strangers that the surgeon had worked from were still attached to the paperwork, features she'd been interested in ringed or indicated by arrows in smudged red ink.

Leaving your job wasn't illegal, and neither was regening. But when you were a ReTracer, and the government had invested a whole lot of time and money in your training, the situation became – complex.

'Can I get madam some refreshment? Tea, perhaps?'

Jude blinked. 'Er, no. Thanks.'

The young man stopped halfway to the sideboard, visibly thrown by this deviation from the procedure. 'Certainly. Right. Then we'll get straight down to business, shall we? Can I ask madam to explain exactly what she's interested in trying? And please, don't be afraid to be specific. The more exact madam is about her requirements, the more likely she is to be pleased with the end result.'

She'd gone for small talk, the first time round. Asked questions she already knew the answers to: did it hurt, how good were their surgeons, how far could they guarantee the results? But she was tired now, a tiredness of some deep part of herself that was following her from body to body, self to self, and her patience was wearing virtually transparent.

'I'm a ReTracer,' Jude told him, 'and I want a full makeover.'

There. Not a reaction, but the absence of one. The surprise, the worry that should have been in his eyes – and wasn't.

'I see,' he said, lowering himself into the chair opposite. The springs creaked faint protest. 'Madam does appreciate that changing any part of her genotype, however small, may have unpredictable effects upon nebulous genetic variables – such as her ReTracing abilities?'

'Oh yes.' Jude found that the dry smile came easily. 'Madam appreciates that very well.'

His mouth contracted into a thin, pale line.

'Do I sense a sudden lack of interest in taking my hard-earned cash?'

The receptionist looked briefly away. 'Madam must also appreciate that what she is asking for is . . .'

'Perfectly legal.'

'In the strict sense, perhaps.'

'Is there any other sense?'

He frowned. 'This is a licensed clinic, madam, not some fly-by-night backstreet operation. Licenses are not cheap, and have to be renewed yearly. If someone in authority decided that we were no longer worthy of holding a licence . . .'

Exactly what he said last time. I don't need to be here. This is all a waste of time.

'That didn't stop you,' she said, 'when Emma DiFlorian came knocking.'

He moved faster than she'd imagined possible.

Bioteching doesn't just change the shape of your nose or the size of your ears. It makes you strong. And fast. And other, scarier stuff. If he'd come at her, in anger or panic, she wouldn't have survived.

But he didn't.

He went over the back of the chair, tumbling it across the room as he rolled, and plunged through the door to the foyer. Jude rose in what felt like slow motion, trying to resolve the blur back into the shape of a smiling man with catalogue eyes, and wondered if there was any point in following.

And then she heard the faint ping of machinery in the foyer and couldn't quite stifle her laughter.

Mr Human Streak here, faster than a speeding bullet and all that, who could have outrun her in any direction he wanted, was taking the lift.

The indicator panel told her where to find him. Nineteenth floor. Of course, if he was smart, he'd have got out of the lift there and hurtled back down the stairs while she was on her way up, using the whole subterfuge to buy himself some escape time.

Jude suspected that he wasn't actually that smart. Which was a pity, because she'd feel a lot happier about going up there if there was a good chance he'd be long gone.

Desperate measures.

What happens if I die here? Will my future just unravel, no falling from windows, none of this ever happening? Will Fitch weep at my funeral tomorrow or the day after, instead of boycotting it in six months time?

In the end, you don't save yourself at all. You just change the date of your death. No one gets out alive.

Ping.

The doors opened.

Blank corridors, still patched with rectangles of bright paint where pictures had once hung. Open doors bled grey light into her path as she emerged. Glimpses of equipment waiting placidly under dustsheets, shelves of papers bleaching slowly in the sun. End of the corridor here. Only one way to turn.

Has the bird flown?

She could hear faint sounds; rustling paper, perhaps, draughts through broken windows. Mice, or worse. Nothing else. Nothing human.

Not good. Smacked of a trap.

'OK, Superboy,' she called. 'Let's be sensible about this. You come on out, without the faster-than-light thing, tell me what I want to know, and I walk away and forget I ever had this conversation. Just anonymous information I picked up off the streets. How does that grab you?'

No reply.

'No, I had a feeling it wouldn't. You just remember, buddy. When they come for your licence. When they fling you in Newgate and all those nice muscleboy Green activists start offering to share your shower cubicle. I offered you a way out of this, you just remember that.'

Still no reaction.

Damn.

Jude started down the corridor.

One thing was for sure. She was going to have difficulty kicking backsides in this skirt. Bloody Schrader and his bloody disguises. 'They'll never suspect you dressed like that,' says he. I'll bet he only wanted to see my legs, the –

Schrader.

The only person who'd been involved in this complex tangle of ReTracery twice. He'd been the one who'd handed her this assignment. Deputising for Warner while he was in a meeting. Was that significant?

Answer: she had no idea. For all she knew, the clue to sorting all this out could be tied to the price of bean sprouts or her mother's shoe size. Too many variables.

Still. The way he'd looked at her on the Millennium Bridge. 'I've been meaning to talk to you for a long time.'

About what?

Movement.

Instinct, unhelpful as always, froze her to the spot.

Yes, there. Behind the door. Very slight, just the twitch of a hand perhaps, or a head. Then stillness, and the shouts of the barge-men on the distant river, bellowing for trade or cursing their steersmen as another collision was narrowly avoided.

Well, she thought, I have two choices. I can stand here until this hideous skirt gives me a wool rash, or I can take the initiative.

Deliberately not stopping to think things through, she hurled herself at the door.

With a terrible grinding of hinges, it slammed into the wall and bounced back at her, throwing her off balance. Something rose from behind it with a screech of terror, flapping and fluttering among the cobwebs. Wings beat briefly, desperately against the window glass. Behind the door, she could hear the faint cheeping of small and vulnerable things.

Finding the missing section of glass at last, the raven launched itself out into the rain, crying out in triumph as it spiralled cloudwards.

And then she saw him – felt him, more likely, registering the movement behind her with older, deeper senses than mere sight. Already gone when she turned, leaving just the blank absence of a corridor newly vacated.

He was still here, then.

'Sorry about the birdbox.'

The deserted chicks twittered panic and were silent, as if she'd somehow confirmed their worst fears.

'You don't talk much, for a salesman. How'd you get this job anyway?'

In the room the raven had abandoned, a box of cleaning supplies was perched on top of a heap of broken furniture. Stepping inside, Jude picked up a broken table leg, hefted it uncertainly. No. No, that was just silly.

Whereas the spray detergent – well, that would be very useful indeed.

Clutching her new-found weapon at her side, she marched back out to the corridor.

How long would you be able to move at that speed? Not long. Even if your nerves were hyped enough to handle it, your heart couldn't keep up the effort. Couldn't move the blood round the body fast enough to feed the muscles. More than a few seconds and you'd basically suffer a stroke.

No wonder he'd taken the lift. He couldn't outrun her. He could use the speed burst to evade her, yeah, but in the long term, all it would do was wear him out.

The next door. Ultramarine light and barricaded windows; she paused on the threshold, waiting for her eyes to adjust. Realising too late that standing outlined against the corridor lights wasn't such a great idea.

Shelves, glass-fronted and reflecting luminous blue. She raised a hand to shield her eyes. Papers rustled in the frigid currents circulating from the wide grilles in the ceiling. Goose pimples rose on her bare arms.

Her reflection stared back at her from the glass: and behind it, something else was staring too.

Shivering, transfixed, Jude moved closer.

It was exactly the way she'd always imagined it. Jars and bottles and tanks lined up on the shelves, a Frankenstienian museum of the unwanted. She leant closer to read the labels. Mrs this. Mr that. Dated last year, this year, years back. Same red stamp on the corner of every label. UNWANTED MATERIAL. Removed to be replaced by something new, stranger, better.

Inside the cabinet, rows of carefully paired eyes stared disfocusedly back at her.

She stepped back and hit the door, knocking it closed. Revealing a whole new dog-leg of the room, flat and depthless in the unsettling light. Square coffin-like tanks on steel benches bubbled with thick, gelatinous liquids, lapping the limbs of hunched and humanoid shapes.

Suddenly, horribly sure she'd found what her past had

summoned her back to witness, Jude edged towards the nearest tank.

The bubbles rose in unbroken columns, blurring the details of the olive skinned huddle behind the glass. Dark hair floated horizontally on the surface, penetrated by tubes and pipes and long steel needles.

As she pressed her cheek to the glass, finding it strangely warm, the creature on the other side shifted in her sleep and turned to face her near relative.

Emma DiFlorian.

Pale and cold and drawing hard on the oxygen mask buckled to her face, while the thick sea-green rose and fell, waves breaking over her shoulders in torture or in healing. Her lips parted – to offer some strange wisdom, perhaps, or to plead – but Jude was already stumbling backwards through the shelves, flailing arms knocking jars of once-precious body parts to shatter on the floor.

Definitely time for back-up.

Crashing back into the corridor, wide-eyed with panic and disbelief, she found that the salesman was trying to get past her.

That was the only explanation for the suicidal headlong rush, the smudge of movement hurtling up the corridor towards her. She froze.

For an instant, his face stabilised, still among a blur of racing limbs, and his dark eyes fixed on hers. Startled and somehow hurt, as if he'd expected something better from her.

Jude raised the antibacterial spray bottle she'd lifted from the cleaning supplies and pumped the trigger.

His head snapped back. Something too fast to resolve hit her in the ankles, the knees. The dark blur slowed and fell. Becoming a body, then limbs. A body she was falling onto as it slid along the corridor, face-up, knuckles ground into eyes, sweeping her feet from under her.

Something hard and flat connected with her back, fell away; an opening door, spilling them into a darkened room. A table leg connected with her ribs, triggering a landslide of papers and coffee mugs and, finally, they were still.

She was lying on his chest, staring into his face as he squirmed and struggled to cough up disinfectant.

That was the other problem with heroics. They hurt.

Swaying to her feet, Jude was astonished to discover that she hadn't broken anything. Not even the stupid pointy heels on these ridiculous shoes. Last time she went anywhere in disguise.

Last time, actually, she went anywhere on Schrader's say-so.

Superboy didn't look like he was going anywhere for a while. In fact he looked sweaty and incoherent, which made sense, if he was suffering from exhaustion.

She went and stood over him, doing her best to exude power and control over the situation. Which seemed to work. He looked dazed, and actually rather happy that she'd taken command. The relief of surrender.

Either that, or she'd misjudged the angle, and he could see up her skirt.

'So. Tell me about DiFlorian.'

'I don't know any more than you do,' the young man wheezed.

'I know she's in a tank down the corridor, breathing jelly, five or six days after you said she'd checked out.'

He rolled his eyes heavenward, as if she'd completely missed the point. 'We told you it – might take longer than usual. Several attempts. She's fine. You have nothing to worry about.'

You.

GenoBond?

My dear employers – DiFlorian's dear employers – dispatched her here and then denied all knowledge, even sent me here to perform some entirely cosmetic 'investigation'.

Time to use a few brain cells.

'So how is the process going?'

'We told you. Difficult. The other two we tested . . . natural ability. Hers is barely half developed, and tweaking a ReTracer's abilities is always a hit and miss process.'

An impossible process, that's what she'd been told; but then a lot of what she been told recently hadn't exactly been the whole truth and nothing but.

Taking a risk, she accused, 'You said you could do it.'

'And we will. You've got to be patient.' He levered himself into a sitting position, shaking his head to clear it. 'You should have said you were here to check on progress. Scared the hell out of me.'

'Trust me, you returned the favour.' Remembering she was supposed to be throwing her weight around, she added, 'Call it a little test of your integrity.'

'Why do I get the feeling I didn't pass?'

'You could have been less conspicuous, put it like that.' And then the words came tumbling out of her, before she'd time to check their plausibility. 'Maybe I should get any paper evidence out of here before anyone puts you to the test again.'

He frowned. 'We said there'd be no paper trail.'

'We said that – but did we stick to it?'

The salesman's doe eyes clouded. 'There's technical paperwork. The lab techs are going to need it if we have to make another attempt.'

'Then we'll hand it back.' She made an attempt to look apologetic. 'Cut me some slack here. If I come back with a couple of sheets of paper to wave at my boss, I've saved the whole project from a dangerous potential leak, right? You know how this corporate shit works. In return, I'll keep your name out of it, and we'll forget you tried to run the twenty-second mile the instant I mentioned Emma's name.'

He looked at her for a moment, taking in the bargain. Appreciating the trouble he was actually in.

'Okay.'

She offered him a hand up.

'By the way,' she said, 'you should consider suing whoever sold you that modification. It's obviously about as much use as eight legs and a tail.'

'Funny,' he muttered, and she couldn't tell if he meant it or not. 'We had someone in for one of those last week.'

The corridor was eerily quiet. Jude wondered idly if anyone else here knew about floor nineteen's dirty little secret. Maybe the whole company was a front for some GenoBond lunacy, and all the staff were downstairs right now shredding the evidence.

What were they doing to Emma DiFlorian?

Whatever it was, it had happened to two people naturally; GenoBond wanted more. She remembered the alley behind Club Andro, and Harchak, muttering darkly about Geno-Bond experiments. It looked like she was going to have to follow through on her promise, if she ever saw that part of her life again.

Secret genetic experiments. Passing information to Harchack's illegal gene clinics. Knowing about a missing ReTracer who was actually metamorphosing in a jar in Dr Frankenstein's lab. Now, doesn't that sound like the kind of thing that could get a girl thrown out of a ninety-storey building?

The dark-eyed man was still out of breath, trailing one hand along the wall as if he really wanted to cling to it for support. Jude wasn't feeling much better herself.

No time for a rest. Get the paperwork, get out. That's obviously what you're here for. To expose this. That's how you save yourself. So just hang on in there, you're almost –

Ahead, the lift doors opened, and Warner strode into the corridor as if he expected to find all hell waiting for him.

Superboy stopped in mid-step.

'Marcus Arturo, I presume,' Warner said, with barely a glance down at the electronic prompter cupped in the palm of his left hand. 'You're under arrest for failing to observe the proper waiting time before making alterations to the DNA of a registered ReTracer.'

The dark-eyed man spun round, poised to run. Jude stepped aside. One head-on collision a day was quite enough to satisfy the terms of her contract.

But he didn't get that far. His knees buckled and he crashed forward, slumping sideways against the wall. With his legs tucked under him, he looked like he'd started melting from the ankles up.

Jude raised one hand in a nervous salute. 'Mr Warner.'

He just nodded uncertainly. Not sure what to say to her.

Or not sure how much to give away.

'Schrader said he'd sent you in,' he announced. 'Rest of the squad are downstairs, turfing out the customers. Find anything?'

'Oh yes. And how. I think we may want to strike a deal here. This man is our only witness –'

The dark-eyed man shuddered and hung his head. Something about the ensuing silence stopped her mid-sentence. It was only when Warner reached her, frowning as he moved her aside, that she realised Superboy was no longer breathing.

'Shoddy workmanship,' Warner murmured. His hand lingered on her shoulder as if he was trying to transmit something to her by touch. 'Adrenaline activated modifications, practically suicide.'

Staring down at the young man's eyes, as blank now as the ones she'd seen in jars, Jude murmured, 'I don't remember that.'

Breaking the Recommendation, damn it.

'I haven't heard anything. About that.'

'Really?' He cleared his throat, only managing to draw attention to his nervousness. 'It's been quite –'

'Did you know that Emma DiFlorian is down the corridor in a regening tank, being modified on the orders of Geno-Bond?'

Panic illuminated Warner's eyes.

'So how about an explanation?'

He took a step back, tugging nervously at his hair. 'We should, I mean, there may be more employees – Back-up, we need –'

'Like Schrader? He's tied up in all this, isn't he? Best of buddies, you two – when it comes to pulling the wool over my eyes.'

'Jude. You can't afford to get involved –'

'Bad luck. I'm already in deeper than you can imagine. So how about you tell me what's going on, before I put you in a jar with your pet project – and maybe without any oxygen?'

Warner's hands fell to his sides. She saw him draw breath for a confession, a speech, an unburdening. She saw the way his eyes grew damp and his lips dry –

And then the shadows swept in and she was hurtling forward again, towards a future where she knew she would still be falling.

FIVE

The Pigsty, eight years ago

'I'm not saying we shouldn't do it.' Farah gripped the safety rail with both hands, leaning into it as if bracing herself against the emptiness. 'I'm just saying that if we're going to risk getting thrown out of training for this, it had better, we'd better get this absolutely right. Right?'

Trembling with sudden vertigo, Jude took a step back from the railings.

Autumn sunlight, slanting and sad, gilded the damp roofs of a dozen abandoned office blocks. Pigeons huddled for warmth, keeping a wary eye out for the birds of prey that sneaked in from the North Downs in search of a quick snack.

The roof of the Stables. That was what the training officers – parade ground sergeants by any other name, putting them through their drills – called it. Claimed there was some reason, a mews or a royal stables used to stand here, but no one believed that.

They – the students, the ReTracers-in-waiting – called it the Pigsty. Full of fat little piglets squealing for the farmer's attention. I'm better than her, faster than him. I can go back further, closer to the crisis point. I can convince those I find there to listen to me. I'm the best little piggy on the farm. Pick me, pick me, pick me.

'So.' Yona fixed her with a challenging stare she'd obviously spent years honing. 'Now goody-girl Farah is all worried about being thrown out of the Pigsty.'

'They won't thrown you out,' the dark haired girl across

the roof from them said quietly, wriggling her bare toes deeper into the rooftop gravel. 'They'll kill you.'

It was Emma DiFlorian. Of course. The pattern was coming together nicely, the recurring parade of people implicated in her present-time crisis. All she needed now was to know how to make it stop.

And that was always the hard part.

'Can't kill us,' Yona muttered. 'Too valuable.'

'With another ReTracer born every three or four months, and the system picking them up within the first five years of their lives almost without exception?' Emma shook her head, like a professor forced to explain herself to a particularly stubborn infant. 'One or two losses are all part of the process.'

Seeing the looks that flickered, oh so briefly, across her friends' faces, the uneasy combination of hostility and panic, Jude had to smile.

They'd been inseparable, Farah, Jude and Yona. The hold-outs. The ones whose parents hadn't noticed their child's peculiar ability to get their own way, after a split second's dead-eyed mental 'absence'. The ones who'd denied it or hidden it or been afraid of it. The ones who hadn't realised.

They were late arrivals, sharing classrooms and exercises with squealing, infantile eight or nine-year-olds. Yona, a Bankside girl herself, had introduced herself in the traditional manner, confronting them both within half an hour and picking a fight. Still confused, afraid and looking for some-one to take it out on, neither Jude nor Farah had bothered to pull punches.

They sat out a week's loss of privileges together, and that sealed the matter. Bestest friends, the graffiti said. Yona, Jude and Farah forever.

'Anyway, I don't think they could if they wanted to,' Farah pointed out, undoing another shirt button as if that would free what remained of her courage. 'We're ReTracers. We could just go back and unkill ourselves.'

Jude heard herself say, 'It's not that simple.'

Emma looked up, grey eyes suddenly narrow with interest, and Jude wondered if she could tell.

But there'd never been a way to tell what was going on in Emma DiFlorian's head, and it wouldn't help her if there was.

Yona grunted. 'We know, Jude. We were in the lectures too, remember?'

'Unfortunately.'

'Yeah. Metaphysics with Boring Bardsley. Do you think he'll ever turn up to a lecture with his pants actually zipped up?'

'Now that really would break the laws of physics!'

They laughed together, high and in perfect unison, the way girls do. The teenaged Jude should have been cackling along with them, but the amusement caught in her throat.

What has this got to do with windows and conspiracy and people trying to kill me? We were children. This was just a prank. We didn't even get into trouble about it, not real trouble.

There's no connection to my future –

Except for her.

Emma DiFlorian, leaning forward now to draw shapes in the gravel with the end of her pencil. Spirals and swirls, the kind of intricacies her leisure time, her world, was made of.

She was tall, Emma, and her hair hung in rats' tails because she didn't comb it much. She spent a lot of time up here, and by now the others probably didn't even notice her. Which was fine, because she didn't notice them. Or the teachers, or the counsellors, or anyone else interested in getting her to participate in training. They knew she had it, the ability, the gift, but no one could get her to use it. The only reason she was still here was because no one knew what else to do with her.

Jude watched as Emma got up and strolled to the far side of the flat roof, behind the rusted water tower. After a moment, she took two steps forward, positioning herself perfectly like a dancer finding her mark, and swung her foot out in a perfect arc.

The gravel shifted before her. Same pattern, different scale.

'They'll stop selling tickets for tonight's draw in just over an hour.' Yona glanced at Jude. Demanding support. 'We don't want to be late, draw attention to ourselves. We have to make a decision.'

Farah stood up, stretching her legs exaggeratedly. Her shoes were new and built up like clogs; the latest, most desperate last gasp of the fashion industry. The beautiful people were neglecting to alter their clothes so often, now they could alter their faces instead, and the rag trade was suffering. And jewellery, the diet business, all the ways people compensated for the body their genes had foisted on them. The TV pundits were talking about imminent economic collapse.

Not that Jude cared. She was fed, clothed, protected. Paid, though she wouldn't get most of it until she turned sixteen. Her mother was out there somewhere – a sudden brutal kick of guilt, quickly suppressed – but her mother was a survivor. Always had been. No need to worry about her.

She swallowed hard, choked by hindsight.

'This won't work,' Farah was saying. 'I mean, we can't just go where we like, right? There has to be a crisis, and we get pulled back to the crisis point? Right?'

She'd forgotten how annoying Farah could be. The way she said 'Right?' all the time. The way she tossed her head to get her hair out of her eyes. Like a horse. Been in the Stables too long and coming over all equine herself.

'Oh, that's done,' Yona giggled. 'I created one.'

'What?'

'I told Ahmed Saxton that Jude had won some money on last night's InstaLotto. Wasn't sure how much, but she looked pretty happy. Happy enough for him to pay her a visit.'

'Yona!' Farah shrieked, sending the pigeons on the building opposite into a flapping, cooing spiral of alarm.

'So, now we have a crisis – or at least, Jude has – and consequently, as soon as she ReTraces, she'll come back here. With tonight's InstaLotto numbers, thus ensuring that we win and have enough to pay off Ahmed.'

Farah pouted. 'The idea, wooden-head, was to get the money for ourselves – not Ahmed and his aggro boys.'

'If we hit the jackpot, there'll be plenty to go round.'

'I don't know. Ahmed has a lot of friends.'

Yona sighed, as if irritated by the questions of a small child. 'If there's any real trouble, I'll have a crisis of my own, won't I? And then I can skip back to the moment I told him – and not say anything.'

'You're sure that won't lose us the money?'

'Of course I'm sure. Unlike some people, I was paying attention in theory class, instead of flashing my chest at Carlos.'

'I was not. It's not my fault people stare.'

'That doesn't mean you have to stare back.'

'It's rude to ignore people.'

'Particularly when they look like Carlos.'

Farah tossed her head again, about to get up and flounce away.

'Of course,' Jude said, 'I could just skip back to the moment before you tell Ahmed, and break your jaw before you even set eyes on him.'

Farah seemed quite amused by that.

Yona scowled. 'And how does that makes us any richer?'

'It doesn't. But it solves the crisis. Going back to the day before I was brought here and running away would solve the crisis. Not being born would solve the crisis.'

'But –'

The sun was giving her a headache. The sun, her friends, and the burden of all the things they didn't yet know.

'You can't rely on when and how the crisis will get solved, or knowing what to do when you get there. Or how many shots it'll take, or what else you'll change along the way.'

Yona was squaring her shoulders for a fight; probably didn't even realise it. 'Well. Hasn't Miss Academia got a piece to say.'

'Miss Academia is being far from academic,' Jude snarled. Hearing the difference in her own voice – the bitterness, the maturity – and knowing they did too. 'And she hasn't finished yet. The heist's off. I can't ReTrace and get the lottery numbers, because this isn't fifteen-year-old Jude you're talking to.'

Emma's foot swished through another arc, dividing the virgin gravel into strange new territories. Order out of chaos.

'Oh,' Yona said, her voice high and thready. 'Oh.'

Farah stepped back as if she'd been slapped.

'And no, I don't know why I'm here. Or what you have to do with the fact that I've just been thrown out of a skyscraper window and I have to find out why before I hit the ground.' Her breath was coming in fierce, shaky gasps. She was angry, angry with them and with herself. 'And for the record, it didn't work anyway. I ReTraced and gave you the numbers, but when the draw happened – second time round, for me – the numbers they drew were completely different. Training Officer Anderson won. Gave it all to a kid's charity. Just to prove that nothing's ever as easy as you think.'

'Who told him?'

'No one had to tell him, Farah. Three ReTracers hitting the jackpot, pretty suspicious. And since he's supposed to stop us exploiting our abilities for personal gain, it constituted a crisis, for him. And back he went, to sort it all out.'

'My head hurts,' Yona muttered. 'My head really hurts.'

'Imagine how mine feels.'

Emma's foot inscribed another section of the ever-expanding pattern. Jude wondered if she'd even heard.

Farah stood with her head cupped in her hands for a moment. Finally, she emerged, her expression locked into a sweaty frown. 'So, you're from the future, right?' A faint grin, a desperate attempt to make meaningful contact. 'Just like that robot movie you're always hunting the schedules for.'

'Yeah. I guess it's true that you turn into what you loved the most.'

'I thought it was me you loved the most.'

Jude hung her head.

The stairwell door slammed shut in Yona's wake, echoing and final. Perhaps she'd gone to report a glaring breach of the Recommendation, or perhaps she just couldn't face the Ghost Of Autumn Future.

'We didn't get hitched, did we?' Farah observed. 'Didn't turn our backs on the capitalist hegemony for the open streets of anarchy and freedom. Or any of that crap you gabble when you're high.'

'No.'

'So what did happen?'

'Farah, you know I can't –'

'Oh no, of course you can't. You can break the Recommendation to tell us how childish we are, how stupid you find us now you're a professional, but you can't tell us anything that matters. Anything that would actually help us get through this place. And if you're so bloody professional, how'd you get thrown out of a window in the first place, eh?'

Turning her back on a question she couldn't answer, Jude stalked across the rooftop towards Emma.

She looked up, briefly. Good sign. The convulsions of a leaf in the wind could fascinate her for hours, but she wasn't usually much interested by human movement.

Then Jude looked down, at the trailing end of a spiral inscribed among the gravel two steps ahead of her, and understood why.

She didn't want her work of art ruined.

'Emma?'

No reaction.

'I really don't have time to mess around here. Let's make a deal. You help me with my little crisis – because I think you can, you keep cropping up in my life for a reason – and I'll warn you about something in your future that, trust me, you're going to want to avoid.'

DiFlorian sighed. 'You don't know what I want to avoid. You don't even know who you're talking to.'

Jude opened her mouth to say the obvious; and then she got it.

'Oh, yeah. You're just here on vacation as well. How are you finding it? Being your child-self, I mean. It's never quite the way you remember, is it? And the food's not up to much.'

'That's not actually what I meant.'

Sitting down in the gravel, Jude fixed her with a hard stare, and settled in to wait.

'The problem is,' Emma said, 'that we can never change our own past.'

'Parallel universe theory? There's an infinite number of universes, and in each one, a version of us living some slightly different life. So when we alter things, we're actually moving into that universe. Nothing ever changes – we just go to the place where that option always was and always will be.'

No wonder my head hurts.

Emma wriggled her toes until flecks of gravel worked their way out from between them. 'Good theory.'

'I think it's nuts.'

'But what I mean is – the past changes for everyone except us.'

Because we always remember.

The UN President was assassinated on his first visit to the Reclaimed Lands. Someone had told her that at a social. Just came up in conversation. Then he'd stammered and blushed and had to retreat to the bathroom, because, for everyone else, it had never happened. He'd ReTraced and made sure it didn't. But for him, it was part of his memory, part of his life.

'How does that help me?'

'It means you know things that other people don't.'

'Because for them, those things never happened.'

Emma nodded.

'But that's no help, if those things aren't of any use.'

'What do you know that no one else does?'

'I know . . .'

I know that Emma here ends up in a jar, being modified into something GenoBond wants and isn't getting – very often – through the normal course of evolution. I know that people want me dead because I know these things. I know that a woman with a bad-taste handbag tried to kill me when I was a kid, though how that connects is anyone's guess.

GenoBond does pass instructions backwards. Someone ReTraces back ten or twenty years to when they first joined, gives the message, and someone in that time-frame takes it back to when they first joined and in the end . . . What if someone wanted me dead so badly that they tried to get me killed before I'd even been spotted as a potential ReTracer? Before any of this ever happened, just wiping out a vast chunk of history – my history, anyway. Who has the authority to order that?

Warner. Oh yeah, I bet Mr Black Espresso can pull some pretty hefty strings within the organisation. But he's never seemed the sort to –

Schrader. Now there's a suspect. But he's just a ReTracer –

kind of senior staff, gets to issue the odd order on Warner's behalf, but surely not powerful enough to . . .

'Parallel universes,' Emma said suddenly, startling her, 'have one big advantage.'

'Yeah?'

'Every single possibility exists somewhere within them. If we keep going long enough, eventually we find somewhere where we weren't born us.'

Something about the way Emma stepped back from the pattern, frowning stern satisfaction at the swirls and helixes, told Jude the conversation was over. She stood up, shivering in a sudden gust of wind.

She'd loved this place. Only realised it once she'd left, of course, because that was how things worked, particularly when you were young and in love and everyone else in the world just seemed to be there to spoil your fun. She'd loved the roof, and the dead-end corridors where they'd played drunken hide-and-seek with no place to hide. And the kids. All the silly, giggly kids who didn't know what they had or who they were or what lay ahead of them, except that, with the optimism of childhood, they were going to get everything they wanted from life, just as soon as they got out of here.

And now she was drawing closer to Farah with every step. Closer to the question still hanging between them, the answer she didn't want to give.

Maybe she didn't have to. Maybe there was another path for Farah, away from the complicated double-crosses and ReTracing to cover her tracks, away from the night when the gang she'd just robbed caught up with her before she'd had time to pop back and erase the trail.

'You know what? I was always so jealous of what you did.'

Farah spared her one-time friend a frown.

'Spotting that share option and ReTracing to tell yourself to buy some. And the day before the Act making it illegal for ReTracers to buy shares went through, too. And McGregor Software! I mean, everyone else thought computers were dead in the water. You made a real killing.'

'Me?' Farah pressed the back of her hand to her mouth to hold in her astonishment. 'Owning shares?'

No, my love. Not in my world. The way I remember it, it was Ahmed Saxton who did the dirty on the Stock Exchange. The training officers were livid. Threw him out, but what did he care? The deal was legit when he made it, hours short of the Act becoming law. They couldn't touch the money.

Jude grinned and winked, and found that her delight was genuine.

'Shares,' Farah sighed, as if Jude had advised her to invest in carthorses or tea clippers. Then that infectious smile cracked her face and she threw both arms around Jude. 'I'll miss you.'

'I'm not going anywhere. I mean, fifteen-year-old Jude will be back in charge of this body the moment I ReTrace. That's assuming you don't break all my ribs in the meantime . . .'

Farah sprang back so quickly she almost fell over. 'Sorry. Didn't – Sorry.'

The sun glittered on the metal heart she wore on a chain around her neck, on the multiple, mostly useless zips scarring her skirt. She seemed to glow from within.

Losing focus. Jude was being pulled back.

'Farah –'

At her feet, the gravel patterns squirmed as if jolted into sentience. Their helixes entwining in an erotic parody of conception, worming into some strange new lifeform. The smeared continents of a hundred thousand infinitely repeating worlds receded from her across the rooftop, alternate worlds she could no longer tell apart.

Emma's eyes met hers as the light flared to swallow her.

'Unless we can find a world where we weren't born us.'

Gone.

SIX

A Party . . .

'– and then I said –'

An elbow jogged her arm; a mumbled pardon, a glimpse of a face punctuated by diamond studs and framed by blond curls, and the woman was gone. Jude blinked down at the champagne in her hand, her strappy high heels, the out of focus carpet below them.

'And then she said,' Fitch finished helpfully, 'you may well be a bishop, but I know a parson's nose when I see one!'

Laughter, fuelled more by alcohol than amusement.

Oh, this is wonderful. Major crisis in progress, life in danger, limited amount of time to save myself, etc. And what do I do? I go on a guided tour of my social life to date. Childhood, tick that off. Adolescence, yup. Big party with champagne and general decadence? Got that too.

Stepping back from the circle of sniggering faces, she tried to turn on her heel. The room tipped alarmingly to one side, righted itself. She wondered if they were on a boat.

'Jude?'

Fitch's hand, delicate and sheathed in lace, fell on her arm. Gloves, how kitsch. How Fitch. Hey, that was pretty funny –

Stop that. Sober up. And stop swaying. People will think you're the dance act.

'I'm fine.' One step. Another. Still upright. 'Just need some air.'

'Well, you won't get any going that way. Come on.'

Leaving Fitch in charge of the steering, she concentrated on the walking. It made things simpler.

Where am I? Whose party is this? Why did I drink this much of their champagne? And why am I wearing these ludicrous shoes?

Images reared from the corner of her vision to startle her. A flower vase, a splatter of red and gold against green walls. A table of shimmering glassware. A familiar face, mouthing words too fast to take in. Light and shadow, groping hands, private huddled conversations in the dark.

She pasted on a smile and tightened her grip on Fitch's hand.

'I know,' Fitch said, as the green gave way to glass and, abruptly, to the narrow metal curve of a balcony.

'You do?' Jude reached for the railings. Cold, wet to the touch. Air's damp too. Been raining recently. Somewhere below, green and brown blurred together, punctuated by the bright mobile sparks of dresses and suits and coats. Outdoors. Nice. Damp.

Closing her eyes, she compared the image against a million billion fragments of her past, cross-referencing in ways her conscious mind couldn't begin to comprehend.

Nothing.

'I meant,' Fitch continued patiently, 'that I know what's happening. I saw it in your eyes. Like you'd just woken up and didn't know where you were. You've done that going back in time thing, haven't you?'

'Shhh. If anyone hears you, all hell's going to break loose.'

Fitch blew air through her teeth. 'It already has. Did you see the cabaret?'

'I'm serious. No one is supposed to know when a ReTracer is –'

'I know that, my love. That's why I bought you out here.'

'Oh. Good point.'

'I never thought about that before. How scary it must be. To suddenly be somewhere else and not know where, maybe, or why.'

She opened her eyes.

The balcony looked down on some kind of concourse. Circular and about twenty metres below. A shadowy intermediate level separated them, flickering with occasional neon. Too quiet for bars. Shops, maybe, after hours?

But this wasn't any mall she'd ever set foot in. Too well kept, for a start. And then there was the fact that the concourse was mostly turf. Shrubs, flowers, and turf. People passing through, but in no hurry. Holding hands, yelling greetings. Happy people, smiley people. And none of them seemed to be carrying weapons, which was the weirdest thing of all.

She looked up. Domed roof, high enough to make her dizzy. The sky outside was that amazing blue that only appears at the moment the sun touches the horizon. As a child, she'd thought something that vivid had to be somehow solid and had climbed onto the window ledge hoping to gather handfuls of it. It was amazing, all things considered, that she'd lived this long.

When she lowered her gaze, Fitch was looking at her with the worried curiosity of someone who suspects an elderly relative is already halfway down the road to senility.

'Since you've guessed my little secret,' she conceded, 'I suppose you may as well tell me where we are.'

'Willington Green,' Fitch beamed. 'Warner's throwing a party.'

Warner? This wasn't his house. She'd been to his house; big lawn, hydrangeas. Inhabited by a grinning wife with a wine glass glued to her hand and a teenage son who seemed more than averagely sulky.

'A party? In a mall?'

'What . . . ? No. Willington Green is a Hurst.'

'Oh God. Tell me I haven't signed anything.'

The 'senile relative' look returned to Fitch's face, just for a moment. Then her face creased with laughter. 'You? Sign up to live in a Hurst? You have to be kidding.'

'That's what I sincerely hope.'

Still grinning from ear to ear, Fitch shook her head. 'It's a party, Jude. Couple of suits are trying the hard sell, but no one's sober enough to give a damn. And you don't think I'd let you sign anything in this condition, do you?'

Crisis over, Jude leaned on the safety rail and took a couple of deep breaths.

Below, a few isolated figures were wandering, consulting maps or leaflets as if searching for something of interest. Whatever it was, she didn't think they'd find it here. The only things here were darkened branches of The Health Factory, and identical rectangles of door and window and fire exit patterning grey walls.

Then she realised the joyous squeaking of the couples below was aimed at those same identikit rectangles, and their flouncy curtains and triple security locks, and realised the salesmen were having more success than Fitch realised.

'Actually,' Fitch said, 'these ReTracer types are all right. Know how to throw a party. I'm surprised you haven't introduced me to them before.'

She forced a smile. 'Wanted to keep you all for myself.'

'Right. Like I'm going to run off with Schrodinger, or whatever his name is.'

A cold knot of anger contracted in her gut. 'Schrader?'

'That's the one. Big blond guy, thinks he's evolution's gift to women. Been sidling up to me all evening, muttering about wanting to talk.'

'I'll bet.' She glanced back at the dying blue of the sky. 'Don't trust him an inch further than you can throw him.'

'Did I look like I was going to?'

'No,' Jude conceded. Taking a moment to examine exactly how she did look, in that black and gold cocktail dress and those gloves. She looked beautiful. And dangerous. As always.

In fact, she looked like an ally.

'How would you feel about helping me out?'

Fitch grinned. 'What, in public?'

'Keep that thought for later. Right now – how would you feel about bringing Schrader out here and having that little chat?'

Fitch scowled like a child threatened with the loss of a favourite toy. 'And if he is just after some horizontal action?'

'Then you're quite capable of throwing him off the balcony. But something tells me that's not what's on his mind.'

'He's involved with this, isn't he? Whatever you're trying to sort out.'

'I'm not sure yet. But maybe.'

Fitch drew herself up to her full height. For a moment, Jude was almost tempted to pity Schrader.

'Okay. Let's go get Mr Blond. You're going to be listening in, right?'

'Eventually.' Jude let go of the balcony and was delighted to find that the world remained still and upright, if slightly fuzzy round the edges. 'First, I have to go find a witness.'

The function room had stopped spinning – very considerate of someone – and the buzz of conversation had dropped to a bearable level. Lots of familiar faces, suddenly pasted onto glamorous frocks and risqué cut-away suits that reminded her of male strip troupes.

Marty the security guard had actually regened for the occasion – ten per cent swarthier and twenty per cent less muscle, by the looks of it. They'd better hope they didn't have a major security crisis before he changed back. Or maybe he was planning a change of career. The way he was handling that voluptuous sixty-something from Accounts, gigolo looked like a good bet.

God, she hated work parties. Come Monday, she was going

to have to look all these people in the eye again, and forget that he'd been found in the toilets with the post-boy, or she'd ended up face first in the punch bowl.

Taking another deep breath, Jude stepped round a seven-foot-tall woman from Genetic Analysis and scanned the room for her target.

'The name's Warner,' she imagined him murmuring to some doe-eyed trainee, somewhere among the crush. 'Calvin Warner, Head of Agent Assignment. Actually a good deal more exciting than it sounds.'

Okay, he probably wasn't busy smarming one of the trainees into bed. Though, judging from the neat pairs of grey suits and bright cocktail dresses to be found in every corner of the function room, he was the only one who wasn't.

He wasn't at the bar either, which did surprise her. That only left the men's room, and she didn't fancy searching that.

Come on. Fitch said she'd give you ten minutes before approaching Schrader – and if he pounces on her before she's ready, she may not be able to delay him.

Schrader had better be involved in all this. If he wasn't, if the line of enquiry she was following was a product of her imagination, then she was obviously headed for a nice relaxing stay at the nearest asylum.

Plunging through the loose crowd of twittering couples hovering in the doorway, she stepped out into the artificial twilight of a Hurst night.

It took her a second to focus – or rather, to believe what she was seeing. To register the neat low doorways and leaded-glass windows, the pastel walls and immaculate window boxes, as something other than an alcohol-induced retreat into childhood. To realise that people actually lived in these toy-box houses, lived and squabbled and got up in the morning to face their neighbours without embarrassment.

Forget Hursts. They should have called them nurseries. A tent fortress for your castle, a womb without a view. Why wait until you're dead to get a box all your own?

Then she heard the whisper of a familiar voice, and realised that she wasn't the only one taking the scenic tour.

The corridor – road, she realised belatedly – was wide, but the strange springy surface didn't seem to be marked up for vehicles. Anyway, in this enclosed and echoing rat-trap, she'd hear even the quietest traffic long before it hit her.

Resisting the impulse to tiptoe, she set off in search of the voice.

The windowsills displayed assorted tokens of ownership, as if the occupants were afraid their anonymous box might be re-colonised in their absence. Children's toys, wooden animal figures carved for a few pence an hour in downtown warehouses renamed Mali or Senegal to give some validity to a 'Made In Africa' sticker. China figures too old and cheap to be anything but family heirlooms; not worth selling, but somehow imbued with too much dark magic, too many ancestors' potential curses, to be thrown away.

She came out at an intersection, where a hexagonal skylight cut upward through layers of identical corridors. Blurs of movement paced the glass, three floors up, or five, or ten. The insomniac inhabitants of the Hurst, taking their dry, mudless, temperature-regulated constitutional? Or visitors, planning out their future? 'Wouldn't this one be just ideal, John?' 'Why, yes, Jane, but so would all the others . . .'

The next stretch of road was bounded by wide expanses of safety glass. Low-level lighting within gave her a glimpse of the interiors: desks and roundabouts, computer terminals and ABC charts. Shaking her still alcohol-fuddled head to clear it, she managed to separate the two worlds, reality and reflection, to opposite sides of the road.

Right hand side, offices; left hand side, crèche. Watch

mummy and daddy at work only a road-width away and ponder that one day, you'll cross the road to your very own desk and chair and peptic ulcer. That's education for you.

Another intersection, heavy with an unnatural silence. Maybe they pump sleeping gas through your air conditioning. Just to make sure you don't have any nightmares about freedom and chaos and wake the neighbours, of course.

Somewhere along the right-hand corridor, she heard Warner's voice say, 'I can't be held responsible for the free choices of my employees, you know.'

Jude grinned. Hold you responsible for anything, Mr Warner? How dare they be so inconsiderate?

'They should,' a precise, embittered voice murmured, 'have been trained better.'

'I wouldn't know. Training has never been my responsibility.'

'That's as may be. The fact is, we are terminally short of travellers, and even one who won't fall into line is one too many.'

'Maybe,' Warner muttered, 'you should try giving her all the facts, instead of expecting her to sign up for a handful of hints and whispers.'

'The moment you give us some reason to believe that she will sign up, she can be trusted with the facts. Until then –'

Warner cleared his throat; halfway along the corridor, Jude froze, suddenly convinced that he'd heard her approaching. 'I need to get back. If I'm not at the commemoration ceremony –'

'Then the world will end, yes. You have an exaggerated idea of your own importance, Warner. GenoBond would be able to go on functioning without you.' His voice tightened slightly, adding weight to a threat. 'After all, one of these days, we'll have to.'

Her heel clicked against a metal plate, a drain cover or

something, and suddenly the tall man was drawing back into the shadows and Warner turned to meet her, as sweaty and over-enthusiastic as a husband who's just hustled his mistress through the back door. 'Jude? Taking a look around, eh? You see, I told you you'd like Hurst living if you'd just give it a try.'

There were a lot of things she could have said to that, but by now Fitch would be well past fluttering her eyelashes at Schrader and onto the real business, and they'd probably missed the good stuff already.

'Mr Warner,' she panted, making it look as if she'd crossed the whole Hurst in a hurry and this was vital and urgent. 'Can you spare a moment?'

His eyes darted to the thin man standing in the shadows, searching for an excuse to say no. The stranger flashed his teeth in what might have been a smile, and said nothing.

'Oh come on,' she protested. 'Don't embarrass me here. These people went to all the trouble of setting up a surprise presentation for you and nothing I can say will get you to it?'

'Surprise?'

Taking advantage of his confusion, Jude grabbed Warner's arm and tugged him forward, away from the shadows and the silent, resentful stranger. 'Come on. If we're late, I'll only get the blame.'

'I'll, er –' Warner twisted in her grasp, firing apologies back at the thin man. 'We'll talk about this later.'

'Mmmmm,' his companion half-agreed, as the intersection corner separated them, and Jude was left trying to decide whether she was going to eavesdrop on the wrong conversation.

Warner tugged free of her grasp, made an ineffectual attempt to smooth the creases from his jacket. 'All right, Jude. What is this really about?'

'We're going to eavesdrop.'

'I see. On whom, and doing what?'

'You have a dirty mind, boss.'

The doorway to the party room was empty now; a sea of grey and colour gathering at the far end, where a short, shrill woman in a dress of silver scales was tapping on her glass, and squeaking, 'Quiet, please!' like a lost schoolmistress. More familiar faces; Miyahara, even, jostling for position, squeezing the miniature video-camera in his fist like a weapon as he battled for the best footage.

What could be going on at a departmental party that a freelance reporter would consider worth recording?

Warner's face creased in annoyance. 'I should be here for this. People take note, you know. My next promotion could depend –'

'Don't worry, boss. If you don't get the directorship, I'll ReTrace back and knock off your rival for you.'

All that emerged from Warner's throat was a strangled sob.

'That was a joke, by the way.'

He was too busy grabbing a champagne glass from a passing waiter to reply.

The crowd was, if anything, getting noisier, but the fish-scaled woman had decided to start anyway. 'It is my great pleasure to welcome here tonight our guest of honour –'

Warner was still gulping champagne and looking unfashionably pale. She reached to pluck at his sleeve, but he stepped back, out of reach, almost knocking over a couple of teenagers in rumpled suits who'd arrived late for the speech.

No more jokes about political assassinations, must make a note of that. Obviously hit a sore spot.

Which might explain why he was talking to a shifty-looking stranger down a side street in Toy Town in the middle of the night . . .

Filing that possibility for future investigation/gossip/blackmail, Jude nodded impatiently towards the door. Warner scowled furiously, and looked around for somewhere to put his glass.

'A pioneer in the primary research field of our century, a man to whom so many of us owe so much of our happiness,' fish-scale woman simpered, stepping back in the humble manner that must be genetically engineered into event hostesses. 'Show your appreciation, please, for Dr Martin Harchak!'

Applause – genuine, for once. Even some cheers. And there he was, thinning hair carefully shaped to hide the bald patches, smart suit hanging awkwardly off his shoulders, managing the thin smile of a man who's won a competition he never even entered. Harchak, petty gang-lord and breeder of wolf-men, last seen bruised and humiliated in an alley outside Club Andro.

Or had that even happened yet?

Warner was moving for the door. No time for curiosity about what the Hursts and their well-manicured guests owed to Martin Harchak.

Back through the party – jostled, hustled, elbowed and grinned at, fending off fragments of greetings and protests and old, old pick-up lines. Nudging Warner like a disobedient sled dog towards the side door, the corridor to the balcony, and the beginnings of some answers.

The corridor was in shadow, and all she could see was two silhouettes, two mismatched profiles against what was left of the light. Shoulders back and jaws raised as if squaring up for a fight.

They were barely going to be in time for the fireworks.

'That's another thing. I wish you'd stop calling me "boss". Makes me –'

'Shh.' She pulled him sideways, keeping close to the wall.

The raised surface of some textured fabric tickled her bare skin, distracting her with false danger signals.

'You have to be aware of that,' Schrader was saying. 'You can't have lived with her so long without noticing signs of instability.'

'Bullshit,' Fitch muttered.

'I appreciate that you have a certain loyalty to her. That's good.' Half a step closer; trying to use his height to intimidate her. Or to look down her neckline. 'But for your own sake, you have to consider very carefully –'

'That Jude's deranged? I've considered that for as long as it deserves – oh, four seconds, maybe – and come to the conclusion that you're lying to me. Now, why would you be doing that?'

She could almost hear the smile in Schrader's voice. 'Well. Perhaps because Jude is a very dangerous woman who, unbeknown to her, has the power to change the world.'

Warner's hand fell on her shoulder. 'Stop.'

'What?'

'You don't know what you're getting into. You're in enough danger already –'

Schrader was speaking as well, but she couldn't take in both conversations at once. Something about the greatest good, drowned out by Fitch's unprintable reply, cut across by Warner, 'We have to get out of here.'

'Why?' Jude demanded, as she followed his gaze to the ripple in the crowd far behind them, the ripple of figures closing purposefully on the corridor, and them.

Whatever's going on here, Warner's trapped, however unwillingly, right in the thick of it.

'You son of a bitch,' Fitch snarled, stepping back as Schrader's hand fell on her shoulder. Lace ripped as she raised her hands, readying those lethal nails for self-defence.

Unthinking, Jude plunged forward. The corridor separating

them was three strides long, three split-second strides, and she was still too late.

Schrader turned his head, just enough to be sure she saw his smile.

And then he disappeared.

In the strictest, Cheshire-Cat sense, slowly but without doubt – disappearing. No melodramatics, no thunder and lightning, no transporter beam from the heavens. Just a thinning to transparency, and beyond, into nothingness.

Jude pressed her palms to the rough cloth of the corridor walls, staring into the afterimage of his insolent grin, and reminded herself to breathe

ReTracers couldn't do that.

Could they?

She turned to Warner, but the world was already slipping away.

SEVEN

A Slip-road, date unknown

The ground went out from under her in the dark, and she fell.

Grass, wet and slippery, greasing her threadbare jeans with mud as she slithered blindly down a shallow slope, thrashing for handholds that didn't exist. Too dark to see, too hot to breathe.

Something hit her in the midsection on the way down, flat yielding metal; she tipped headfirst over it and landed, coughing her lungs up, in a ditch full of waste cellophane and weeds.

Quite an entrance.

She sat up, rubbing her lower ribs absently. She still seemed to be in one piece. The object that had stopped her headlong was above and behind her now, stark against neon-smeared clouds. A roadside crash barrier, knotted with bindweed, flaking rotten paint into the wind.

She could hear distant traffic. Probably just over the embankment opposite. The low, steady hum of a motorway, not the hiss of frustrated engines in suburbia.

No traffic here, though. Just tarmac and wilted grass and litter. Slip road to nowhere. Nowhere she recognised, anyway.

All right, no need to panic. It was only to be expected, a little – disorientation. After going back so far, changing so much. Considering the chaos she'd already wrought in her own past, this could be any anywhere, any day of her increasingly alien life.

She looked up, hoping to catch the phase of the moon – for what little use that would be, but any scrap of information would be reassuring right now. But there was no moon. Just sodium-light glare on the road signs – DRIVE CAREFULLY, WE WANT TO SEE YOU AGAIN – blotting out the stars.

Clutching at the crash barrier like a drowning woman, she hauled herself upright, and sat down on the cold metal to examine her surroundings.

A single lane road, cracked by the heat, the advertising embossed into its surface dated enough to startle her. Munchie-Crunchie, for goodness sake, who ate that these days? The print was faded to near-invisibility; probably old news, even in the here-and-now.

She sat for a while, hoping for a car with a blaring stereo, a bus with current advertising, anything to tell her when she was.

The traffic noise over the embankment ebbed and flowed, but no one took the Road to Nowhere.

Wandering out into the empty expanse, Jude blinked at the logos for a moment. Then she turned to face the fairytale glitter of the far horizon.

Ulti-Mall.

Four perimeter towers, vast petals of mother-of-pearl not quite concealing the machine-gun emplacement, glowed with a soft internal light. The walls, silver and ebony and turquoise like the city in Revelation, the one she'd liked hearing about because it was pretty, and all those dragons and beasts sounded like fun. Lasers etched the company logo onto the low cloud; a ring of currency symbols, dollars and Nu-marks and all sorts. Dissolving slowly, the way the customers' account balances did.

Everything exactly the way she remembered.

She'd been able to see the towers from the windows of the

Casaritto apartment, the one Mum cracked into the housing department computer to requisition. The one they'd been thrown out of six months later, when the internal security program had finally disassembled her access alias.

Nice apartment – as nice as they could manage without drawing attention – but Jude had been fourteen years old and more interested in the fact that you could see the towers of consumer heaven from the bathroom window.

That must have been the day Social Education came for her, the day they were thrown out. She'd just met Sharmina – premature teen rebel and more of a flirt than any thirteen-year-old had a right to be. Beginning of a beautiful friendship, that had been. Until Social Education turned up.

All she could remember was crying herself to sleep in a tiny bleak room in the Pigsty, cleaner than she'd ever been in her life, unsure if she was crying because she'd lost Sharmina, her mother, or herself.

Bastards.

The low hum of an approaching engine reminded her she was standing in the middle of the road. At least that meant someone was still alive round here, she realised, hopping back over the crash barrier as the headlights rounded the corner. Let's hope they're just customers.

Ulti-Mall, the biggest single development in the world. Eight thousand shops, a hundred hotels, parking for half a million cars. People came from the cities, the Hursts, from all over Europe. Mostly for a week; you couldn't do it justice in less. And then there were the health farms, the theme parks, the entertainments . . .

It was also renowned as the best place in the western world to pick up rich wastrels with interesting sexual tastes. She hadn't tested the theory herself, but GenoBond employed all sorts, and with all that surveillance equipment lying around, no one kept a secret for long.

She'd been a couple of times, back when she first realised that a ReTracer's salary attracted a high enough credit rating for her to be allowed in. Best clothes, best manners, sweating with nerves as she paid off the taxi and stared into the shimmering brilliance of the entrance hall.

It was disappointing, just as she'd expected. It was flashy, and sleek, and seductive, everything she'd wanted while staring from that cracked window into the luminous night; but inevitably, she didn't want it any more.

Of course, conspicuous consumption brings its own problems. A hard core of beggars began haunting the perimeter ring road, displaying their ragged children like begging bowls. Ulti-Mall generally turned a blind eye to them. Some of their patrons enjoyed salving their consciences by tossing a handful of foodstuffs from the rear window as they passed. The ensuing battle among the starving was considered amusing.

The car-jackers proved more of a challenge.

They'd started subtle. Weeping women in expensive suits flagged down cars, or children lay still and bloody on the slip-roads. The concerned driver got out, and someone leapt out of the bushes and drove the car away.

But Ulti-Mall was concerned for its reputation, and once the security patrols widened their boundaries and started shooting to kill, the situation escalated rapidly. Now the jackers carried heavy hardware and preferred not to leave witnesses.

Seeing the approaching headlights begin to slow, Jude had a feeling that the local gang were about to get lucky.

It was a small family model, company issue; pretty low-key, for someone on the way back from Ulti-Mall. As it drew level with her, still decelerating, Jude realised she could no longer hear the engine.

It came to a halt a few metres beyond her and, in the sudden silence, she heard the clicking of the ignition and muffled voices. The headlights died, and the internal light came on.

A young man driving, an older man in the passenger seat. She couldn't make out their faces, but their body language said confused rather than worried. Which puzzled her. If she'd had an engine failure out here, at night, she'd be soiling herself by now.

What puzzled her even more was that the boot and the rear seat and all the other spaces that should have been full of Ulti-Mall goodies, were quite plainly empty.

Old guy and young guy were exchanging ideas. Any minute now, they'd get the manual out. Or the mobile. Either way, it was going to be too late. With the internal light on, they were blind to the shifting shadows, the nebulous movements in the distant scrub.

Absolute sitting ducks.

Keeping her jacket pulled tightly around herself to deaden the giveaway glow of her white shirt, Jude watched in guilty fascination as the car-jackers circled closer.

They were good. Keeping low, moving gently, taking their time. It was only the slight advantage of distance and angle that revealed them to her. From the car, they'd be invisible until it was too late.

What has this got to do with me? I don't even know these dimwits.

Or maybe I do. Maybe they're people I know in a new face, a new body. I hope I don't associate with anyone dumb enough to break down on an Ulti-Mall sliproad and not panic about it, but . . .

Or maybe I don't know them, not yet; but once I get back to the present, I'll find that all the changes I've made have brought them into my life, made them vital to me. Made them the key to changing all this. I can't take anything for granted, not any more.

I wonder how many times I can ReTrace before I hit the ground?

The wind was picking up, agitating the gorse and the clumps of escaped bamboo, hiding the quick scuffling movements in the scrub. But the older man had already noticed something was wrong. He said something, sharp and afraid, and reached up to snap the interior light off.

The young man turned, lifting his chin as if affronted. A gesture that seemed strangely, indefinably familiar.

Blinking in the gloom, Jude shifted position, trying to pinpoint the car-jackers.

One there; big, clumsy-looking male, with a stick or a cudgel. In the bushes, keeping low. Waiting for the others to catch up.

Skinny woman off to his left; a gun in her hand, probably a revolver. War souvenir, traded cheap in a glutted market. Common as stones.

Oh, and behind her, two girls. A family business. Cute. One in her teens, the other seven or eight, both identical; long-haired and lean like ancient warriors, slinking through the veldt to surround their enemies. She wondered if they'd ever known any other life. Were car-jackers born to the trade? Birthed in a burnt-out people carrier, weaned onto car snacks, playing 'jackers and marks instead of doctors and nurses?

The girls looked like they might scare off, if she made a lot of noise. Mummy and Daddy wouldn't, though. You could tell that just by looking at them. Pros with years of experience, and the scars to prove it.

I can't believe I'm even contemplating taking these people on.

But then, this is my past, my future, my life at stake. What choice do I have?

Shifting position, she felt something heavy inside her jacket. Cold metal, smooth plastic.

Drawing it out, Jude found herself staring at the knuckle-duster silhouette of an army flash-stunner.

ReTracers weren't licensed to carry weapons. The bosses said it would make them lazy. And this was hi-tech, the sort of thing she'd only seen while on duty around government ministers or other bodyguarded VIPs.

Forget how it got here. It evens the odds, that's all that matters.

She slipped her fingers through the grip. The metal bar rested easily across the outside of the hand, glowing faintly, *that's right, and all it takes to fire is a definite clenching of the fist . . .*

The smaller girl, her dress torn and hair disarrayed, had emerged from the undergrowth and was looking around as if lost.

The old lost child routine. It was nice to see the ancient traditions being kept up.

'Mummy?' she asked the empty road; then turned towards the car, demanding of its occupants, 'Please, mister, have you seen my mummy?'

Yeah, kid, I've seen her. About three metres behind you, loading that hand-held blunderbuss of hers, and if I can only get a clear shot –

Inside the car, the younger man leant forward, across his companion, and opened the glove compartment.

Mummy car-jacker reacted instantly. Nothing like the maternal instinct. Snapping the revolver back together, she levelled the weapon at the front windscreen and fired.

Glass shattered, and the older man jerked backwards, his back arching and relaxing like a dummy in a crash video. She heard the crack as he fell forward, head first, against the dashboard.

In the silence, the young man gulped air, a big scared sob of it. Then the headlights came on – dazzle them, smart move, maybe he wasn't a hopeless case after all – and the horn started blaring, and the car-jackers broke cover to rush him.

Feeling uncomfortably like a figure from a comic book, Jude raised herself onto one knee, pointed her fist at the skinny woman and squeezed hard.

There was more recoil than she'd imagined possible from something that only emitted light. Or sound and light, or something. She should have paid attention to what that nice bodyguard was saying, as well as to her figure. Her arm jolted back like someone had hold of her elbow, and the flash swallowed everything.

When Jude finally managed to open her eyes again, Mummy car-jacker wasn't there. But whether that was because she'd keeled over, or just dived for cover was anyone's guess.

Everyone was in battle mode, breath-baited silence. Bright sparks bounced around her field of vision, making it hard to distinguish figures in the gloom. The little girl was running – down the road, away from her family, which had a ring of truth about it. And there was her sister, still on the job, settling into cover under a bush.

Hoping the flash had dazed everyone else as much as it had her, Jude scrambled to her feet and bolted.

The crash barrier was her only cover – that, or the car, which was too well lit by the streetlights for her liking. So, they'd expect her to move up and down behind the barrier, sniping at them.

Not to head off up the open slope.

Streetlights only lit the road. The embankment was in darkness. If she kept quiet until they showed their faces again, she could catch them from an angle they hadn't thought to cover.

Down on the road, the door of the stalled car sprang open, and the young man hurled out like half of hell was on his tail.

Idiot.

Looked like she'd have to modify the plan.

She dropped, arms folded over her neatly-cropped hair (she'd never had her hair that short, was this version of Jude DiMortimer born without fashion sense?) as the firing started.

Teenage daughter, this time, with a semi-automatic. Very odd, because car-jackers wouldn't be firing in the direction of the car if they could help it. The tank might be empty, but there'd still be enough petrol in the system for a big loud bang if a bullet penetrated the wrong area – and all the valuable Ulti-Mall goodies were still inside.

Looked like someone was paying the ladies and gentlemen of the road to move into what were now delicately referred to as 'final visitations'.

When GenoBond had told her that stopping assassinations was part of the job, this wasn't what she'd had in mind.

Somehow, the young man had made it to the barrier unharmed. Now he was worming his way underneath, into the litter and the briars, making the most of what cover he could find.

And look, there goes Daddy. Trying to circle the car and cross the road unnoticed while his target has his head down.

Telling herself it was easy, this sharp shooting business, Jude aimed the stunner at the girl in the undergrowth and squeezed the grip.

Lightening arced behind her closed eyelids. When she managed to open them again, she could hardly see, and she was getting cramp in her fingers, but there were no more gunshots.

In the ditch, the young man was squinting up the embankment in search of his guardian angel. A little reflected light played across his face, picking out sharp cheekbones, a small, firm mouth.

He was hauntingly familiar.

Daddy car-jacker had come to a halt in the tall, straggly weeds near the opposite kerb, unsure whether to continue the hunt or turn back and minister to the casualties.

Jude rolled sideways, supporting herself on her free arm, and gave him three flashes from the stunner.

He landed face down on the tarmac, his makeshift weapon rolling away into the clogged gutter.

She could slip away now. Leave the young man to explain himself to the security patrol, doubtless already on its way. Make the news, not that she'd ever see it. Mysterious superhero strikes on Ulti-Mall approach road, wielding a flash stunner and wearing badly cut jeans . . .

'Hello?' the young man called, shielding his eyes against the false-dawn glow from behind the embankment.

Hello yourself.

Maybe I should say something. Do something. Maybe he can't trust the police either, maybe I've come here to do the traditional thing – snatch him from danger, go on the run together, bond, save one another's lives, even get smoochy?

No, thanks, big guy. Mind you, you do look so familiar. There was that boy at school; what was I, eleven? Had to have a boyfriend. Everyone else did. He didn't mind walking me home, sharing my lunch table; he had his eye on the football captain. Boy's team, that is. What was his name, anyway?

The young man cleared his throat. 'We don't have all night. What are you waiting for, a password?'

She tried to smother her laughter, but it didn't work. He heard her and stood up, smoothing his shirt-tails in a gesture she recognised at once, as he yelled, 'What the hell is your problem?'

'Fitch?'

He turned towards her, head cocked, trying to locate her from that half-formed whisper in the dark.

Behind him, Mummy car-jacker raised her head from behind the thorns and levelled the revolver at his back.

Jude brought the stunner up level and squeezed, but she knew it was far too late. The shot was already ringing in her ears, the frail-faced man in the nice suit was staggering, falling, and there was nothing she could do.

Instead, she ran.

Down the slope, finding footholds among the broken glass and discarded numberplates without conscious thought. Light reflected from the palm of his hand, upturned to the sky. Her knees buckled and she was kneeling at his side, her hands stroking hair from his eyes and knowing the feel of it, the smell of familiar shampoo even, and tears welled faster than she could blink them away.

He coughed. Very carefully, as if he feared to disturb something. Jude struggled to recall some scrap of first aid, some clue gleaned from one of the many fatalities she'd witnessed and then reversed. Nothing came.

'There was a girl,' the young man wheezed, 'used to call me that.'

'I know,' Jude managed. She took his hand in hers, found it sticky with blood. Gluing them together.

'Stop the bleeding,' he wheezed. 'Medical kit. In the car. Got to get the message. To Judith.'

Judith? No one calls me . . .

'Tell her they're coming.'

'Who's coming?'

He coughed again, spraying a fine mist of blood onto her sleeve. 'She knows. Believe me, she knows.'

'All right. When are they coming?'

The young man's face crumpled into silent laughter. 'She's – ReTracer. What does "when" matter?'

'I'll give her your message. If you tell it to me, clearly –'

The non-stranger turned his head so his cheek rested against her hand. 'Schrader.'

'Oh, not him again. And?'

The young man's eyes fluttered closed.

'Not yet. The message.' His breathing sounded wet, spluttery, and she knew that wasn't good. 'Fitch. The message. For Judith.'

'Year Zero. Stop them. Before they catch her. Schrader. Only ally. Warner.'

'Schrader is her only ally? Or Warner?'

Another breath, in hissing slow motion.

'Come on, Fitch!'

Another.

'Fitch. Whatever your damn name is. Come on. I need to know.'

Silence.

'Bastard.' Jude moved to rub her eyes, found her hands inexplicably flecked with blood. 'I needed that. I came halfway through my own life for that. But no. Your timing always was appalling.' Her throat was tight with the grief of old mistakes, mistakes that had never even occurred in this reality, but she had to keep forcing the words out. 'Can't even die on cue, can you? Oh, Fitch.'

And the future flew up to meet her, and she fell.

It's a dangerous thing, to be in the midst of a deep and powerful emotion at the moment you ReTrace. A very dangerous thing.

It's so easy, you see. To be pulled off course, to go seeking the emotion and not the time-and-place. To lose your way.

And if you happened to be thinking of a person . . .

EIGHT

Fitch's Place, a few weeks ago

'I didn't tell you,' Fitch was yelling as she stormed into the bathroom, leaving a trail of talc on the carpet, 'because to any normal person, it wouldn't matter. Why would it? Except to you, of course.'

Jude looked down at her hands, and found that they were shaking even more than they had been the first time round.

Just her luck. The one chance she had to go back and repair the worst mistake of her life, and she had to arrive five minutes too late to stop herself saying those stupid –

'Morphophobe!' Fitch was screaming. She'd left the bathroom door open and Jude had to strain to pick out her voice among the hiss of running taps.

'What?'

'Morbid fear of shapechanging. You see, there's even a technical term for it.'

'That makes me feel so much better.'

'It's about time you face up to it, Jude. Get some help. Get with the real world, for God's sake! Just because you're stuck in the flesh you were born with doesn't mean the rest of us have to be.'

Jude looked round the sparse, dusty living room, taking it all in for what might be the last time. The threadbare velour sofa and mismatched chairs, the grubby rugs, the line of cheap candlesticks queuing along the mantelpiece. The bead curtain over the window, salvaged from a deserted pub off the Court Road. Stray items in a ragbag of memories, most of them faded beyond reliability by alcohol and early morning hazes and love. Her past/future, blurring together in the butter-coloured light of a city evening, begging her to remake them, and do a better job of it this time.

She cleared her throat, readying herself for lies, damned lies, and maybe even the truth. 'Fitch. I'm sorry. Can we just forget that the last few minutes ever happened and start again?'

'No, we can't.' The taps cut off abruptly. 'I am never going to forget this conversation. Never.'

'That's what I'm afraid of.'

A moment, then Fitch came to the doorway and stood there, in her underwear, with one hand on the doorframe and the other wrapped around herself as if holding something in. She looked like a photo-model, posing Shock and Disgust.

Jude looked at her and realised she'd run the taps to cover the fact that she'd been crying.

'I'm sorry.'

Fitch's gaze moved around the room, as if she had a lot to do and couldn't decide where to start. But she didn't move. She just stared over Jude's head, waiting for her to say something that would undo the last few minutes – or alternatively, terminate the feelings they'd shared for the last few years.

If Jude knew how to achieve that first option, she would have done it by now. She was too scared of accidentally achieving the second to risk anything uncertain, and so they just stood there in the heat-hazed room as if the silence and the sun had turned them to stone.

Oh, it had started well enough. Warner had called her in at lunchtime for some dull assessment program, questions and stress level tests and round pegs in square holes. She was the only one being tested that day, and even the woman supervising looked bored. Another set of figures to be filed away, another space in another box of paperwork filled up.

No one had any idea how ReTracers did what they did. No one could isolate a single gene or bottle a single altered protein that would allow them to replicate the effect. But the tests went on.

Pretending a doctor's appointment, she'd slipped away early, bargained with a stallholder on a street corner for a rare bottle of Australian red, and walked up towards Politiville.

It had a real name, but no one used it; the area had been Politiville ever since it became the haunt of politicians, barristers and the other chattered-about classes, decades back. That continual influx of money had enabled it to preserve a fragile charm, founded around neatly fenced squares, Victorian lampposts and the few scrawny ducks in the canal.

After the Migration, this bastion of urban gentility had fallen to the tower block dwellers, red in tooth and claw. But it had worked its magic on some, and the rest had simply looted and moved on. Those who remained were optimists to a man, struggling to better themselves and their defiantly hostile neighbours through hard work, neighbourhood pride and flower beds.

At the turning to Fitch's street, Jude passed a gang of them, clad in cast-off pinstripes, hacking up the garden of a collapsed house with shovels and pick-axes.

'Planting pears, don't you know,' one of them shouted, vaguely recognising her, or thinking he did. 'Devon Farmhouse.'

She took a perfunctory look at the bundle of saplings waiting under the defunct traffic lights, just to be polite, then smiled and hurried on. If she expressed too much interest, they might ask her to join in.

Fitch's square had also fallen victim to their creative urges. The central lawn had become an allotment, and fruit trees had replaced the long-rotted oaks beside the stream, shedding unseasonal blossom into the road. As she picked her way to number 37, recognisable by the defiantly non-productive front garden, all dead leaves and wilting lupins, apple-blossom settled bridally on her shoulders.

Fitch was sitting on the doorstep, in something that might have passed for a bikini if it was a little larger, taking in the afternoon sun.

'Someone will report you to the Good Neighbours Committee, y'know. Going out dressed like that.'

'The Committee can go swivel,' Fitch yawned. 'And I'm not out. This is my doorstep. I can do as I please.'

For a moment, she actually sounded angry, then she stood up, noticed the bottle under Jude's arm, and demanded, 'Going somewhere?'

'Only to regale the woman I love with alcohol, laughter and tenderness.'

'Nice idea. If I hadn't agreed to work an extra shift tonight.'

Leaning in against the doorpost until they were face to face, close enough to smell Fitch's lavender perfume, she murmured, 'Who said I meant you?'

Fitch tried to smile, to show that she knew it was a joke, but somehow the smile got twisted in the making, and she abandoned the effort and turned to go inside. 'Come on in. I still have to get dressed.'

'Really?' Jude muttered, trailing into the gloomy hallway. 'And I thought you were going like that.'

'Down Club Andro, I doubt they'd notice.'

Fitch stopped in the bedroom doorway, struggling with the catch on the bikini top, and turned back to her. With that definite 'I've decided, I'm really going to say it' look that Jude had seen so many times from so many others, and she almost knew what was going to happen next.

'I'm glad you came by, because I have something to tell you. I've been thinking about it for a while – I mean, I've enjoyed it, and all, but you get bored with everything after a while, you know? I've decided to book into a gene clinic next week for a switchback.'

For a moment, the word just hung there between them, devoid of meaning. And then Jude found the strength to say, 'Switchback to what?'

'To my birth gender,' Fitch said, as if it was obvious. 'To being male.'

And now here she was, halfway through this all-too-familiar argument, knee-deep in deja vu. Nothing to say – and no need to, because Fitch was doing a great job of holding the argument all on her own. She'd just got through the rant about her rights and now she was started on Jude's narrow-mindedness.

'All you're thinking about is yourself, not whether I'm happy. '

'So are you? Happy?'

Fitch scowled, as if she found that somehow impertinent. 'I was.'

'But you're not now.'

'It's not you, Jude. It's not us. I just get bored, you know?'

'I've lived in this body my whole life. I'm not "bored".'

Fitch shrugged. 'You can't miss what you've never had. You've never had a real chance to try anything else –'

'And I never will. I can't change sex, size, skin colour. I can't reinvent myself every five minutes. All I have is this body. All I have is me and you.'

Biting her lip, Fitch looked away. 'I can't stay like this forever just to please you,' she said.

'Why not? Why bloody not? Aren't we happy? We're happy, we're compatible – what more can you want than that?'

'There you are. That's you all over – expecting everyone else to want what you want. To be content. Well, I'm not going to be just "content". Not now, not ever.'

And that was it. The argument. Like a car on a fairground ride, crashing down from the heights into the dull deceleration of the final straight, knowing the only way to go is back round again.

'Are you going to say anything else,' Fitch demanded, 'or are you going to leave so I can get ready for work?'

'I'm not leaving. Not until we've sorted this out.'

'Fine. You shout, I'll dress.'

'I'm not going to shout,' Jude sighed. 'And I don't think you should go into work tonight.'

Halfway to the bedroom, Fitch looked back over her shoulder, lipsticked mouth pulled into a tight red pout. 'What do you want me to do, lose my job? So I can't pay for the operation? Too late, baby.'

'That's not what I meant.' Jude followed her to the bedroom door, nudged it open. Lavender and old carpets and the dying geraniums on the windowsill mingled with the apple-blossom air seeping through the open window. The single wicker chair in one corner was packed with cast-off clothes, and the heaped tsunami of bedclothes was about to swamp another pile. Fitch stood in the centre of the room, naked to the waist, staring at her reflection as she adjusted the side-zipped leggings.

'If you switchback,' Jude began, struggling not to emphasize the word, 'won't you lose your job?'

'Yeah.' Fitch snatched up a maroon top that didn't look big enough for a doll and thrust her head decisively into it. 'And guess what? I consider that an advantage.'

'So it doesn't matter if you get fired for not turning up tonight?'

Fitch's head appeared through the neck of the top with

an audible pop. She wriggled into the brief lace sleeves, tugged at the waistband in the vain hope it might descend to somewhere near the top of her leggings.

'I need to meet my op broker,' she said, and for the first time the anger left her voice and she sounded uncertain, even scared. 'Miyahara knows someone who can set me up with a cheap deal.'

'Miyahara? You'd take a recommendation from someone with that kind of taste?'

'He got what he wanted. Why shouldn't I?'

Jude watched the muscles of her lower back shift as the top edged lower and lower down her delicate frame. 'And what is it that you want?'

Fitch snorted and looked away.

'No, I'm serious. Who is this new Fitch going to be? Torso by MuscleMan and hardware from the Donkey's Danglers company?'

'Jude . . .'

'One yard or two, sir?'

'Just shut up.'

She turned back towards the mirror, and Jude saw that she was laughing.

'Look, Fitch. What I said –'

'Was the truth. Which is good. I like to know where I stand. No, hear me out. You're a Luddite. That's cute, I admit it. But I can't fit in with all that. I won't spend the rest of my life as one gender, one race, one shape. If everything's there for me to try, why shouldn't I try it?'

'Because,' Jude managed, 'if you can be anything, then what's really you?'

Fitch shook her head, as if the question had no meaning. 'I have to go. Enjoy the wine. In fact, take it down Ludgate, that's where all the unmodified hang out these days, isn't it? All the Luddites in their ugly, deformed, birth bodies, breeding their ugly bastard babies to swamp us. I bet you can find a real woman down there –'

'I don't want a real woman. I want you. Don't go to work tonight. Ring Miyahara, tell him you'll meet your broker somewhere else. I'll come with you. Or not. Anything you like, just don't go.'

She'd run out of breath, had to gasp to fill her empty lungs again, while Fitch stood there and stared at her like she'd grown horns.

'Please.'

Fitch took a step back, shaking her head. 'I know you mean it now – but tomorrow, and the day after?'

'I'm a ReTracer, Fitch. I've been to tomorrow and all those other places. I know what's there. That's why I came back.'

Well, there goes the Recommendation . . .

'To make sure I got it right this time.'

Across the square, the ducks were squawking blue murder. Probably someone looking for a square meal and hoping their neighbours wouldn't notice. Eating the local status symbols definitely qualified as anti-social behaviour.

'You're telling me,' Fitch murmured, low and shocked, 'that you've already lived this moment, you screwed it up, and now you've come back to try again?'

'That's not quite –'

'What am I, an arcade game? Keep trying options until you find the right button to press?'

'It's not like that. I wouldn't –'

But Fitch was backing towards the door, as taut and wary as a cornered animal. 'And you say it's all my fault. While you've been manipulating me, trying out tactics, altering things until I do exactly what you want. Making me into some kind of puppet.'

'It's not like that.'

'Isn't it? How would I know? You could go back and

persuade me not to switchback – take the idea out of my head before I've even really had it. How do I know that anything I've done since I met you was really my idea at all?'

'Now who's being a Luddite?'

'Changing my body, that's my choice. But changing someone else's life . . . Yeah, maybe you can make me change my mind. Fix up all the problems, design me exactly how you want me. But it won't be the real me you get. It'll never be the real me again.'

'Fitch –'

But she was already out in the street and running, lost in a snow of leaves and apple blossom.

Jude looked around the house one more time before leaving. She felt cold, and a little guilty, like a voyeur who'd broken in and didn't know what to do next. Sometimes she did this in strange locations, took a good look round, just to help her find her way if she ever had to ReTrace back. Maybe there'd be another chance –

To manipulate, to change things, pull different strings?

Fitch was right. It was all just pressing buttons.

Closing the door firmly behind her, she tiptoed over the blossom and out into the street.

Well, Jude, that was certainly a job well done. You screwed up bad the first time round; the second time, you screwed up just as badly, but with far better intentions. Well done.

She wanted to ReTrace, to just get away from the gardens and the ducks and the sari-clad women who watched her from the upper windows. But she couldn't, not yet. It wasn't time.

It wasn't over.

She turned into a different side-street, hoping it might kick-start the process. That was all it took, sometimes; leave the house a minute early or late, choose a different breakfast even . . .

Fitch was right. I don't live my life, I play it. Like a game. With everyone around me just a character in my never-ending soap opera. When I was a child, I played make-believe, wrote myself into some great heroic epic in my head; now my life has become a story. The ultimate Grand Narrative, with me as stage-manager, pushing everyone else here and there to make sure I'm always the only one in the limelight.

Movement behind her startled her back to alertness. Someone was walking down the main street she'd just left – dead centre on the empty tarmac, like she always did. Like they'd been tailing her, but hadn't taken the sharp left when she did.

She glanced back, more from curiosity than fear.

A woman in a purple-red shirt and tattered jeans, with unevenly heeled boots that made her limp a little as she walked.

A woman exactly like her.

Too shocked for caution, Jude stared.

She couldn't see her double's face, not from the back. But the clothes were exact, and the hair. All perfect. But misty, like a ghost; precise but transparent.

Looking down at her own hands, Jude realised that she could see straight through to the traffic instructions on the tarmac below.

Reality was splitting, and big-time.

No one else seemed to have noticed. Not the kids bolting across the main street with a shop dummy suspended between them, there one moment and gone the next. Not the woman emerging from an open doorway, drawing a gun from her handbag –

Suddenly, horribly certain of what was about to happen, Jude turned and walked back out into the street.

And, twenty yards away, Jude version Two was looking up, startled, as she heard the safety come off the gun:

Jude screamed.

And maybe Jude Two did too, but the sound of the shot covered it –

And that was it. Shot, bullet, *Jude Two backflipping onto the dirty road, arms flung out like a tumbling trick gone wrong* –

Jude just stood and stared.

I'm dead.

The woman stepped forward, out of the shadow of the house, keeping the gun levelled at Jude's head. Dead Jude, once-and-future-Jude –

What was going on here? Reality can't split like this –

Not for more than an instant, just to show you the path, *You can't be dead and not dead all at once, but she was, and now the woman was cocking the pistol again* –

And Jude remembered her face.

The face of the woman who'd ambushed her on the Side-Ride, fifteen years or a few hours ago. Little Miss Leather Shoes and Matching Handbag.

Looked like she'd finally managed what she'd been planning, all those years ago.

Looked like she was a ReTracer.

Only she couldn't be, Jude realised, transfixed by the cold-blooded execution being played out before her, because she'd have been in her own body back in the Bankside, looking whatever age she was then – and she didn't seem to have aged one millisecond since.

Little Miss Handbag raised the gun again and emptied the magazine into dead Jude's chest

And Jude took a step back.

And it felt like she was falling.

NINE

Interlude

Dying, Jude thinks as she falls, is not at all how she'd expected it to be.

It reminds her of that old film; an old, old film, a slot-filler in the small hours. The woman in the children's playground, looking up and seeing the whole world going up, genuine nuclear Mutual Destruction Assured, the wind screaming through the swings and nowhere to run, nowhere to hide . . .

That's right, it's the one with the woman pursued through time by the killer robot. She'd always felt a peculiar sympathy with that one. The future's like that. It blames you for things you haven't even done yet. It hates you for making it, for all that you had no choice.

Nowhere to hide, nowhere to run.

Welcome to the Fairground of Fun, the Turnaround of Time. Hop on the roundabout, spin from future to past to never-was. Round and round the ReTracer goes, where she stops, nobody knows . . .

Adrift.

This was the possibility they never talked about. In the training sessions, the monthly briefings, even the bars and coffee shops and corridors, where everything from underwear upwards got discussed wholesale. They all knew it happened, but no one ever –

'Jude!' her mother's ghost-voice screams, carried on a shimmer of cheap perfume from the vertiginous blur that edges the roundabout of her life. 'I'll come for you. I won't let them keep you in that place. I promise –'

–talked about it. Because they didn't want to face up to it. Didn't want to admit that it could happen to them. Deny it, and it'll never happen.

Okay. Stop panicking, and you'll find a way to solve the problem.

You're Adrift. You've lost your bearings, slipped off the solid walkways that link your present and your past, down into the cracks in between. What you see before you is your life, flashing quite literally before your eyes. You have to find a stable point – somewhere, anywhere – and jump at it. ReTrace to it. Then, from there, you can get back on track.

And you have to stay calm. Because it's the panic that destroys people, the uncertainty that haunts them when they finally find their way back with their sanity in shreds. Stay calm and you'll be fine.

Of course, if it is simply being Adrift that rips your mind apart, then the damage is already done – so why worry?

'We're offering you a vocation,' Warner says, somewhere out there in her distant past. 'A career. A future. Exercising the most extraordinary gift mankind has ever known. We're offering you something to live for.'

It's not too late.

I hope.

Among the whirlwind, Fitch was crying out, in passion or in pain. Jude folded her hands over her ears, trying to squeeze the memories out of her field of vision. It made no difference. It was all inside her head, all part of her, and there's no escaping from yourself.

A glimpse of the empty streets of the Bankside, the one time after the Migration that she'd gone back. Broken glass in the scorched frame of the SideRide, litter rotting in ghost-town alleys. Even the rats had left.

She reached for it. Felt the chill of steel under her hand as she rattled the locked door of Block 24 –

Gone.

She had to find something solid. Take shelter in a definite event of her life, and ReTrace her way from there. The next hint of a place and time that seemed accessible, that seemed real, she had to make a break for it.

That was what the others had done, the ones who'd made it back. Because some had. It was possible. She'd seen a couple of them, at the Retirement Home. And look, out among her jumbled memories, there they all were. Huddled under their blankets as the nurses brought them tea and smiles. Still riding the whirlwind in their minds, blank eyes reflecting the lamplight, fidgety hands playing out their journey in shaky Morse Code as they recited mantras and poems and nonsense to keep the whirling memories at bay. There. Something solid, something real.

Go.

TEN

The Past

Light. Dark. Light.

Something obscuring her vision. A flap of cloth, a curtain? Warmth behind her, flesh-warmth. She tried to turn. Held too tight, held by giant arms that squeezed resentment into her even as they protected. Her head felt strangely heavy and something was very wrong –

'Hush, Jude,' her mother's voice whispered, heavy with echoes. It came from somewhere above her, somewhere high and distant, yet vibrating –

Vibrating through the glossy plastic of her mother's raincoat. The plastic where Jude's baby-fat cheek rested, the plastic swathing the arm that held her. A raincoat the size of a bedsheet, a tent, damp with mist as her mother carried her, a babe in arms, through the patterns of light and dark that were the night-time city.

She opened her mouth to scream, but all that came out was a baby's cry, thin and weak and inconsolable. Her mother squeezed her tighter, bent close: a blur of skin, the strange, exaggerated movements of her mouth as she hummed and hushed a child who was not a child at all.

I'm a baby.

I'm helpless. I can't even change my own nappies, let alone my own fate.

A car horn blared. Her mother scurried for a few steps, cursing, and slowed again. Muscles tensing and relaxing; a jolt now as she shifted the weight of the helpless bundle in her arms.

Forcing herself to relax, to take stock of the situation, Jude looked down at herself. Flounces of knitted blanket bundling a frilly dress. And little woolly booties kicking vaguely at the night. Isn't that cute?

I wonder what I look like?

No hair, eyes like marbles, and I scream all the time, probably. All babies are like that. Though it is weird that there were no photographs. Even the unwanted usually get photographed at this age. It's only later that the family album develops amnesia, missing out chunks of a family or a life.

What if I need to take a piss?

Okay, just calm down and think.

Lights flickered at the edge of her vision. Green to amber, amber to red. Traffic lights. Working traffic lights. Been a long time since she'd seen any of those. The sharp tang of petrol, the off-key blare of horns, the affronted yells of pedestrians losing brief, hopeless battles for priority. Engines revving in time with the pulse, voices rising and falling to weave a peculiar urban melody.

The thin drizzle caught the light strangely, filling the streets with a glittering mist, reflecting back the colours of the garish window-displays. Adult faces loomed in and out of the light, unnaturally close, grim with internal struggles that no one would expect her to understand.

She could see her mother's face quite clearly. Younger than Jude remembered her, and softer. Thinning hair tied back, but edged with a halo of loose strands that glittered gold in the hazy light. She was wearing make-up, and her inexperience with it showed. Heavy on the mascara, light on the blusher. Some skills, or lack of them, obviously did run in the family. She was wearing blue, a solid, aggressive blue that didn't quite go with the bronze chain around her neck. She looked very determined, and more than a little afraid.

She'd never seemed the sort to take midnight walks with her infant nearest-and-dearest – and though begging with a babe in arms is the oldest trick in the book, she was never the type, and we're moving a little fast to be working the crowd. So where are we going?

The scent of baking bread drifted past, sudden and mouth-watering. And that's another thing. I hate milk. I don't want to be stuck here when dinnertime comes around; my stomach's already rumbling.

Why have I ended up here, in the most helpless phase of my life?

Darkness, sudden and suffocating. Jude squirmed ineffectually for a moment before realising it wasn't any part of her mother blocking her vision. They'd entered a building. White walls, black walls; a blur of light reflecting on glass; the dulled echoes of voices and faint music. Petrol smell fading to chemical flowery-freshness, the thin chimes of elevators arriving and departing somewhere out of sight.

Another voice, close and vaguely familiar. 'Is this the child?'

'No,' Jude's mother murmured. 'I left my daughter at home and nicked this one out of a pram on Wardour Street, what do you think?'

Jude managed a small gurgle of a laugh. Her mother looked down at her, startled.

The tall man in the doorway didn't look surprised by this preternatural occurrence. He just made a note on his clipboard before stepping back out of her line of sight. 'You did come here of your own free will, Ms DiMortimer. No one can force you to give up your child – even when such a bright future awaits her if you do.'

Her mother's grip tightened convulsively. 'I came to listen. That's all. No decisions.'

'Of course. Won't you come through?'

A shift in the quality of light; a dim room lit by wall lamps, bright Art Deco points of light. An expanse of cold grey metal swam into focus as her mother sat down. A table, conference-style, separating her from the blurred outline of a red-haired man.

Give up your child?

She never told me she even considered this. All right, it's not the kind of revelation they advise in parenting classes – 'Did I mention, Jude dear, that I nearly gave you away?' Not exactly reassuring, but things like that have a habit of slipping out. And what's all this about a bright future? Did they know, even then, that I was a ReTracer?

And how could they have? I couldn't even speak, let alone –

Oh, think about it, Jude. People who can travel backwards through time, passing messages back through the organisation to the appropriate year. I'll bet GenoBond know which babies will turn out to have ReTracing abilities before they're even born.

'Ms DiMortimer,' the red-haired man said, 'Life's been hard for you, hasn't it?'

Her mother snorted amusement.

'It's a difficult business, bringing up a child on your own. You've also had disagreements with the Housing Department, and a continuing lack of gainful employment, various legal difficulties and squabbles . . .'

'Yes. I wonder who I have to blame for all that?'

Teasing him? Or is that what she really believes? Was she, well, unstable, even this early on, and I never noticed?

'Hmmm.' He made a note on his clipboard.

'Another black mark, I presume?'

He blinked.

'And if I ask too many awkward questions, is there a box marked PARANOIA for you to tick? Or do you just hit the emergency button and the men in white coats rush in and drag me away?'

The young man bit the end of his pencil. 'As I was saying. Life has been difficult for you. And now, with the Hurst programme approved and the upheaval that's liable to cause –'

'Not for me.'

'I'm sorry?'

'It won't cause me any upheaval. Because I'm not going anywhere.'

'Well, that's your choice, Ms DiMortimer. Though I have to say, bringing up a child in the place that the city's liable to become after all, ah, stabilising influences have pulled out, that's going to be . . .'

Her mother smiled. 'A child's dream come true, yes.'

'Perhaps. But not everything that a child wants is good for them.' He looked a little relieved, as if he'd finally wrenched the conversation back on track, got the upper hand again at last. 'GenoBond, however, always places the long-term welfare of the child at the centre of its plans. If you were to agree to place Jude in the programme, she'll be placed with a loving foster family, have the best schooling imaginable, and training to assist her in developing her talents –'

'You'll stick her in a greenhouse, with all your other little prodigies,' her mother's voice was tight and toneless. 'And weed her out if she doesn't grow the way you intend, I'll bet.'

'Now, Ms DiMortimer, that's not true at all.'

Jude's mother sighed. 'You wouldn't last five minutes on the streets, would you?'

'I'm sorry?'

Pushing a stray strand of hair out of her eyes, she began, 'First rule of trading – you have to have something that the other person wants. And what have you got that I want?'

'With respect, it's your daughter's wants and needs –'

'Me, Jude, whoever. What are you offering us? Pretty dresses and expensive toys? I can get those. Cut-price, traded, stolen. They're just commodities.'

The tall man had turned an interesting shade of purple. Mum often had that effect on the minions of authority. 'Obviously,' he said, 'the benefits are rather more than financial. Her education –'

'You're planning to use her as an inter-dimensional messenger. Why would she need an education? What use is geography and geometry, when all she has to do is turn up and announce the future?'

He cleared his throat again. 'Ms DiMortimer. I can't help but feel that you're being deliberately awkward.'

'I'm asking sensible, logical questions. You're failing to answer them. That doesn't inspire my confidence in you as a fit person to take care of my child.'

'I appreciate that you have a great deal invested in Jude's future, emotionally, I mean –'

'Of course I do.' Almost a growl, full of submerged anger. 'She's my daughter. My own – and only – flesh and blood. And I'm going to do everything I can to care for her and protect her – from you and your plans to turn her into a state-controlled robot, and from anyone else who'd try to harm her.'

What happened, mum? How did we get from this to twenty years later, living a few miles apart but separated by a wall neither of us knows how to scale? If anyone knows, it's the mysterious red-headed man here. Shuffling his paperwork; shifting gears in his head, trying to decide which tactic to adopt next. 'You do realise,' he said finally, 'that GenoBond has a lot of influence, and if we chose to, we could make life very difficult for you.'

This explains everything. GenoBond wanted me reared their way, parented by company wage-slaves and indoctrinated from the cradle to the company pay-roll. But my mother exercised her inconvenient legal right to say no. And that's when everything started going wrong for us.

The jobs that never materialised, the apartments we were evicted from, the deals that didn't work out. Always waiting for her to crack, to take a step over the legality line. And one day she hacked into the housing department's computers to get us a roof over our heads, and the police swooped in and took me away.

Movement; an earthquake of shifting muscles as her mother stood up again. 'I don't think you have anything we want. I shouldn't have come.'

'But we're offering –'

'Stick your offer.' The red-haired man was swept from Jude's view by the curve of her mother's arm as they turned away. 'My daughter is no one's slave.'

Looking up into her mother's face, Jude smiled the brightest, most approving smile her baby muscles could muster.

And then her grip on reality slipped, and the whirlwind sucked her back in.

ELEVEN

Location Unknown

'– bringing you the latest news; city-wide, country-wide, world-wide. Today's headlines: Romanian right-wingers told to get with the action as regening on demand is passed by a majority vote. Crime up, police presence down. Could there be a connection? And – forget film, the new generation of entertainment is here!'

Jude sat bolt upright in bed, left arm swinging out automatically to slap the SILENCE button on the clock-radio. Her hand passed through mysteriously empty air and tangled in soft draperies before hitting something solid, reawakening old pain in bruised, raw knuckles.

She opened her eyes, and immediately wished she hadn't. Not that it wasn't a nice room. The white satin drapes around the four poster were slightly parted, offering her a limited view of the mock-georgian furnishings, heavy velvet curtains, an opalescent washbasin with brass fittings. Fantastic: but what would a girl like her be doing sleeping here?

Jude tugged the drapes open, revealing the radio – a big old brass thing with mahogany inlay, as solid as a police response tank and twice as expensive. Mystified by the array of dials, she eventually found the volume dial and turned it down to a low buzz that combined unpleasantly with the ache at the base of her skull.

There was a creased trouser suit flung over the back of a chair, a briefcase and heavy, expensive-looking watch on the seat. That certainly looked like her idea of getting ready for bed. Wardrobes and hangers were an alien concept to a Bankside girl, who rarely had more than one change of clothes.

The problem was that the suit wasn't hers.

No, she corrected, leaning across to finger the fine weave, assessing the cost with the professional precision of a street-corner pawnman. The real problem, Jude DiMortimer, is that you've never set foot in a hotel this expensive in all your born days.

The real problem is that you have no idea when or where you've ended up.

Her stomach turned over and she barely made it to the washbasin in time to bring up the evidence of yesterday's transgressions, primarily blood and bile.

The towels in the shower-room bore the legend IMPERIAL PARADISE HOTEL in English, German and Japanese, which told her something about the clientele. It also worried her severely, until she remembered the radio announcer. English, and English only.

Good. GenoBond doesn't tend to get involved in overseas operations, and I can't see them paying to fly me home from God knows where.

She took a good, long shower, hoping that somehow everything would dissolve in the spray and she'd wake up somewhere sensible, rational; preferably in bed with Fitch, and right now she didn't much care if that was pre- or post-operation . . .

But she came out of the cubicle to the same pristine tiles and complimentary toiletries, and the dull, shamefaced realisation that she was going to have to call the emergency number and tell them that she was Adrift.

Not least because she didn't have the money to pay the hotel bill.

The speed with which the connection clicked together and

the phone began to ring told her she wasn't far from home. On the city limits, maybe. Her window looked out over a flat expanse of greenery, far too large for a park. Did they have luxury hotels in Hursts?

'Warner,' the low familiar voice growled. 'Make it snappy, I've got a barber's appointment.'

'It's Jude.' She cleared her throat, trying to force her voice down to a sensible register. 'Jude DiMortimer.'

Silence.

'Mr Warner?'

'Ah,' he managed, hoarse with astonishment. 'Jude. It is really . . .?'

'Of course it's me. Who'd want to imitate a life like mine? Just listen. I'm in a lot of –'

'Jude, where are you calling me from?'

'Just listen, right!' Jude gulped at the can of ginger ale she'd found in the near-empty minibar. 'I was in trouble. I got shot. While I was ReTraced –'

'Jude, you can't –'

'I don't have time to worry about what I'm not supposed to tell you. Just listen. Someone killed me. But not me, because reality had split. They shot and killed the other me, and I ended up Adrift.'

Ambulance sirens wailed a long way off, filling the silence.

'And now I've fetched up in a four-poster bed in some hotel I've never even heard of, let alone visited. I don't know where I am, or when. I think – I think I've died in my present, and I can't ever go back. And I'm scared.'

'All right,' Warner said softly. The tremble in his voice was fading, which had to be a good sign. 'It's going to be all right. Things like this have happened before. We don't publicise them, no point in alarming people, but they do happen and we always sort them out. I just need you to get a grip and help me to find you. Can you do that, Jude?'

Shivering in the armchair, bundled in a hotel towel, tears withering her cheeks, Jude didn't feel at all sure that she could. But she snuffled and croaked 'Sure,' and Warner seemed satisfied.

'Right,' the soft, calm voice said. 'How are you physically?'

'All right. I think. I threw up. And I have bruises. But nothing serious.'

'And you think you're in a hotel.'

'The Imperial Paradise Hotel.'

'Oh, sure. I know. The administrator's daughter had her divorce party there. Real classy.'

'I guess.'

'That's the difficult part over with. Now, listen. There's been another separatist bombing on the Ring Road, the traffic's shot to hell. It might take us a while to reach you. So sit back, take a long hot bath, order breakfast, whatever. We'll pick up the bill when we arrive. Well . . .' Warner managed a forced, feeble laugh. 'Within reason. Don't send out for, ah, paid companionship or anything. There's a limit to what GenoBond considers reasonable expenses.'

Lightheaded with relief, Jude found herself laughing in unison.

'Just one thing, Jude. Do not, under any circumstances, leave the hotel.

'With all this on tap, why would I?'

'Indeed. But with recent developments, you could be in considerable danger. You'll be fine as long as you stay in the hotel, but –'

'Yeah. I get the idea.'

His voice tight with strain now, struggling to mask his true feelings and failing miserably. 'I should get people making calculations. You know, to get you back where you started from. What year did you say that was?'

'I didn't – but it was May in twenty-seven.'

'Twenty-seven,' Warner echoed. 'That's twenty-seven After Migration?'

'No, it's twenty-seven B.C., what do you think?'

'Okay, don't get touchy. We'll be there as soon as we can. Oh, and steal me some that violet-scented soap they put in the washbasins, huh? Jenni just loves it.'

'Sure thing, Mr Warner.'

The phone hummed mockery as she replaced the receiver.

The suit was more flattering than she'd expected, and by the time she'd slicked her hair back with a tube of scented gel and opened the curtains to a bright, powder-blue spring morning, she was beginning to feel slightly more in control.

'Breakfast,' she told the auto-waiter, slamming her thumbprint on the sensor pad to add it to the bill. 'Something easy on the stomach.'

The panel pulsed green and red for a moment, sorting the key words and searching for an appropriate stock response.

'May I recommend the Continental? Coffee, chocolate and orange juice with croissants, a selection of sweet and dainty breads –'

'Yes, fine.'

'Anything further?'

'Yes. A newspaper. Uh, *European Times*. That's all.'

'Thank you for making use of me, madam.'

She laughed like a drain at that, but it was cold laughter, queasy with fear.

Warner was a bad liar.

Nothing particular, nothing obvious, just little mismatches, little mistakes. The fear in his voice, the way he didn't even seem to recognise her name.

Which meant there was another reason why they didn't want her to leave the hotel.

Could be innocent enough. She'd been close to hysteria

for a while there; maybe he was scared she was losing it, about to wander off in a daze, or flip into paranoia and start running from the very people trying to help her.

Or perhaps his badly concealed interest in the year 27 After Migration was the key.

The auto-waiter hatch opened with a discreet ping and Jude bolted back across the room, driven by something more desperate than mere hunger. The breakfast tray smelled like heaven, and she scooped up the cup of chocolate with her left hand as her right closed on the newspaper. Proving this was a classy hotel, one that didn't expect you to read your news from a video screen.

Shaking out the single fold, she held it to the light.

Good thing heart disease doesn't run in the family.

February 27th, said the date under the ornate header. February 27th, 32 A.M.

She walked for a long time. It took her mind off things.

The perimeter fence wasn't guarded. Wasn't even electrified. A quick scramble took her over the edge onto a path surfaced with crunchy fragments of industrial slag. A few hundred yards brought her to a bridge, and a slippery, winding stairwell down to water level.

The canals. Some old, many built about the same time as the SideRide, to tackle freight-related pollution. They'd been about as popular as the SideRide, though less compulsory, and the Migration had finally rendered them obsolete. However, their creator's grand plan had not gone entirely to waste.

The towpaths and bridges formed a vital network of short-cuts and escapes that traversed the whole city – if you had the nerve, and the contacts, to pass safely through the territories of the Water Gangs.

This was going to be her "safe" – inverted commas essential – passage home.

Picking slag fragments from the soles of her boots, Jude tottered under the bridge to look for the map. In the shadow of the sodden, mouldering brickwork, the tick of falling condensation followed her footsteps like echoes. She paused a few feet in, allowing her eyes to adjust to the light flickering in undulating patterns across the underside of the arch.

Yes, it was stupid. She knew that. Walking straight back into a city full of GenoBond's allies, servants and paid informers. A city full of strangers who'd sell her, alive or dead, for a pittance, and so-called friends who'd probably betray her without charge.

But the countryside was an Abomination to her. The countryside was open and green and windswept and bare, devoid of territories and boundaries. The countryside was a place of Hursts, model communities packed with smiling people with important jobs and action-packed social lives, people who had everything planned and timetabled and organised, and she didn't belong.

Not to mention the mantraps, barbed wires and officially non-existent army patrols dedicated to 'neutralising' any New Earthers, loafers or Green sentimentalists out there littering the pristine landscape with their messy little lives.

Down on the waterline, something moved.

Jude froze: the brain-dead panic of the fatally exhausted. A montage of unpleasant possibilities, many of them physically impossible, strobed through her mind.

Whatever was in the water turned over with a sodden splash. Light reflected across its dead white eyes.

She bolted.

A hundred yards up the towpath, gasping and stumbling, she turned to look back at her pursuer.

It was a dog. A big, shaggy thing, German Shepherd going on Great Dane, salt-and-pepper fur greased with detergent residues and algae. A little blood remained encrusted around the bullet hole in its skull; as it bobbed unsteadily along the canal and drew level with her, she noticed the raw wound in its spine where the loyalty chip had been torn out to prevent the Animal Militia tracing the owner. They had a variety of ways of punishing negligent owners, and most of them were fatal.

Unwilling to travel in its company, Jude forced herself to walk faster.

A mile further on, the canal spilled over a ruinous lock into a larger, faster waterway, creating a bubbling system of rapids laced with barbed wire and half-submerged bicycles. The dog had vanished into one of the automated cleansing filters at some point between her anxious, haunted glances back at it, and though there were occasional stairways up to street level, there was no sign of the locals.

Now that she was certain of her surroundings – the meandering trunk route pretentiously christened The King's Waterway, decades after anyone laid claim to any kind of kingship – Jude stopped in the middle of a vandalised picnic area to finish breakfast.

The area must have been pleasant, once. The dilapidated houses had long, thin gardens that straggled down to the towpath, full of lime-leaved trees that showered her with tiny white blossoms. Beyond, unfamiliar buildings were rising on the skyline. Greens or cultists were the only people who actually built in the cities any more, but these looked far too professional for them. Maybe the gangs were going respectable, investing in property. It had been five years, after all. Anything could have changed.

Except by the canals. Frozen in time by the neglect of the gangs controlling them, they were falling prey to time and small-scale predations. Here and there, looters had cut archways through the fences and, on departing, left breadcrumb trails of rusted tools or dropped and discarded junk.

Among the damp paperbacks and torn stockings, she found a copy of *St James Infirmary*, rotting in the leaf litter. The Louis Armstrong version, hardly his kind of material. Still, everyone makes mistakes.

She crouched to pick it up. One side had melted onto the tarmac, and it snapped as she lifted it, leaving her staring in annoyance at a jagged fragment of history.

She gave it a sea burial in the canal, trying not to think about the dog.

The bread rolls were still faintly warm and she'd had the foresight to finish off the minibar. A couple of mouthfuls of neat vodka, and a few moments dozing in the sun, and Jude began to feel that she had everything figured out.

It wasn't more than a couple of miles to Deep Ground. She had friends there. Big, dangerous, gene-engineered friends with bad reputations. She'd pulled an illicit job for them, accompanying their leader to a gang meeting, then ReTracing to just beforehand to tell him which trick clauses to look for and what his enemies really wanted. They'd really made a killing, the second time round. They owed her.

Certainly a change of clothes, and maybe an escort for protection while she went over to Fitch's apartment, just to find out –

Fitch. The subject she'd been avoiding all this time, the ghost at the edge of her vision.

It was five years since Fitch had decided to switch back. She could be a man, a woman or a Tyrannosaurus Rex by now. She had five whole years of memories that didn't contain Jude – as a lover, an ex, an enemy, anything. Probably thought Jude was dead, actually. And now the ghost of her dead lover was going to waltz in the door and spout Re-Tracer jargon to explain a five year absence.

And what if she's still a guy, Judey? What do you do then? Close your eyes and think of England? Get her to change back – maybe now and then as a birthday treat, dressing in female flesh like it was sexy lingerie?

Can you live with that?

Something vast and silent descended from the heavens behind her, blocking out the sun.

She was running, instinctively, blindly, before she'd even registered the downdraught and the monotonous clip-clip-clip of the rotors. The first thing she took in consciously was that it was her name the loudspeakers were blaring – stay where you are, you will not be harmed – and that was all the impetus she needed.

'Jude!' Warner's voice screamed over the rotor noise. 'It's me! Don't be a fool!'

Hell, she thought, plunging into the nettle-filled ditch that bordered the gardens, why break the habit of a lifetime?

Something shattered on the rubble behind her, spraying the backs of her legs with a cold acrid liquid. In the split second before the brisk wind flicked the gas away into the canal, her eyes filled with tears.

The wire fence to her right was ripped along most of its length – welding torch, the looters round here didn't piss around – and the lower half had long since collapsed into a tangle of steel and ivy. Ducking under the long strands of melted and resolidified metal that trailed from the top half, metal lianas in an urban jungle, Jude threw herself headlong into the nearest garden.

The ground dipped sharply, a brief slope barbed with thorns and broken glass, and she crashed head-first into a heap of rotting vegetation. Pain lanced through her shoulder. Gasping, she recoiled, spitting dust, scraping leaf-mould from her eyes.

And froze.

Hydrangea leaves, forced vertical by the helicopter downdraught, shivered against her cheek. The silvery underbelly of the pseudo-helicopter was almost close enough to touch. Looked like GenoBond had finally got that budget increase. Brushed metal, sleek and brand-new, peppered with inactive jet nozzles. Better hope they didn't fire those up while she was underneath . . .

Huddled over to muffle her heartbeat from their sensors, she waited.

The undergrowth was thick, woody, heavy with leaves. It would take more than a helicopter's undertow to flatten it and reveal her. Of course, the disturbance might not be enough to mask her if she started crawling for the house. But if she stayed here, they'd start on the tear-gas and trank bombs and all their other toys, and they'd have back-up troops headed here by now, ground-pounders to flush her out.

In the narrow, echoing sound-trap of the canal, the rifle shot echoed like a bomb blast.

Jude jumped like a scared kid; froze again, feeling sweat forming between her shoulder blades. Dammit, they weren't supposed to be shooting at her. She wasn't a danger, so why . . .?

Two shots later, she realised that they weren't.

The echoes gave it away. Too sharp, too far from the original retort. Whoever was firing that rifle was a considerable distance away, firing towards her. Which probably meant they were firing at the helicopter. The prospect of having a ton of blazing metal come down on her head didn't cheer her significantly.

Swallowing curses, Jude began edging forward through the shrubbery. The stench was appalling. A lot of things had died in here, recently, and she didn't want to consider exactly how. There was a thick layer of something wet and slippery under her right knee, inflicting further atrocities on the suit.

She didn't dare investigate. Her stomach felt quite delicate enough as it was.

The next couple of bushes were thick with long, dry thorns. This was all going to get very unpleasant.

'Jude,' the loudspeakers blared. 'Think about this. This area is full of crazies. Gun-freaks, drugged-out gangs, all kinds. Your only way out of here alive is to come with us.'

More shots. Two or three guns now, coaxing a symphony of echoes from the houses and the high crumbling walls bordering the canal.

'Come on, Jude. You can't sort this out alone. You need our help to get home. We can cut a deal, whatever terms you want. I've always kept my word, Jude, you know that.'

Easing through a man-trap of thorns, Jude was wishing that she'd paid more attention during Comparative Religion and Philosophy classes. This seemed like a good time to take up praying.

'Damn you, Jude,' Warner's voice crackled, mere inches overhead. 'You just can't make it easy for yourself, can you? All right. Have it your way.'

The loudspeaker cut out with an audible snap, and the pressure on the shuddering canopy began to ease. The helicopter was pulling out.

Or pulling up, at least, out of range of the sharpshooters. Which ought to keep them occupied for long enough –

Doubled over, keeping herself at least level with the vast mutated rhododendrons, Jude ran.

She hit the rear door still running; cheap plywood rotted by the pervasive canalside damp, which caved in under the impact, spilling her into a gasping heap on the cracked red floor-tiles.

It was a kitchen. Or it had been, a long time ago. Blinking, she could make out the play of sunlight across a cheap tin draining board, the shimmer of condensation on flaking emulsion. A child's picture, faded beyond recognition, was still pinned above the stove, inscribed with damp blurred letters, MUMMY.

Picking her footholds carefully, Jude eased herself upright. The furniture had been overturned in the scramble for loot, and the floor was encrusted with tiny brittle shells of pasta, a random mosaic set in a plaster of rats' droppings.

Clinging to the table legs and drawer handles for stability, she managed to negotiate her way through the filth and out into the hallway, where there was less guano, more light, and more destruction.

Most of the stairwell ceiling had come down, vast chunks of plaster smashing through stairboards or exploding into delicate flowers of white powder on the hallway carpet. The front door stood slightly open, admitting a shaft of the peculiar yellow light that always precedes a storm. The decorative panel at its centre had been smashed in, but the frame was still edged with fragments of coloured glass, chartreuse and cornflower blue.

Keeping flat against the hallway wall, presenting as little of herself for a target as possible, Jude peered out into the street.

Houses. Just like she'd expected. Inner-city suburbs, rotted and forgotten. Broken tumble-down houses and burned out corner stores and –

Rising defiantly above the rubble scattered across the next crossroads, the low Art Deco hump of an Underground station.

Even gun-crazies respected the Underground. And Warner's people wouldn't follow her down there. Not unless they were feeling certifiably suicidal. All she needed was something to trade.

Like the watch currently weighing down her left wrist.

Oh, and there was the small matter of getting there alive. But, as Schrader might have said, little hiccups like that were all part of the excitement of being alive.

Schrader, she was beginning to think, didn't know shit.

Thunder rumbled in the east and a sudden brief rush of cold air announced the arrival of the rain.

TWELVE

'How are you paying?' the eyeless man seated behind the improvised ticket barrier asked her, scratching absently at a shaving cut under his chin.

Glancing round the white-tiled emptiness of the Underground ticket hall, Jude dropped the watch into his outstretched palm.

'Hmmm,' he said, paying the strap between his fingers like a rosary. 'Nice.'

'I thought so.'

'Steal it?'

'It kind of fell into my possession.'

One of the black-clad muscle boys loitering at the entrance to the Excess Fares booth strolled forward, heels clicking on patched concrete, summoned by some signal she'd missed. Jude tensed, wondering how good a weapon the almost empty briefcase would make. But the muscle boy just accepted the watch from the ticket man and strolled away to hand it in over the counter. Safe keeping.

Turning the white scar tissue of his eye sockets towards her in a gesture that was obviously supposed to repulse her into accepting the offer, the blinded man murmured, 'Five tickets.'

'Oh, come on. Eight, at least.'

He blew air through his teeth, already bored by the ritual. He was young, for this job. The ferrymen were pretty crazy, even by the standards of post-Migration gangs, but they didn't usually accord their soldiers the honour of blinding until they were too old to carry a gun. Maybe skinny here had shown a real talent for surfing the tangled currents of the spirit world, or whatever bullshit they were spouting these days.

Lucky him.

'Six,' the blind man said wearily, extracting a sheaf of pale green tickets from under the desk and fanning them like a card-sharp.

'Deal.'

'Rip-off' would have been closer, but she didn't have the time or the energy for the normal process of prolonged haggling. She wanted to be well away from here before Warner persuaded any of his people to change into civvies and tail her. Assuming he employed anyone that reckless.

At least she'd bought herself some time. They wouldn't try anything down here. But then they wouldn't have to. All they need to do was follow. She'd have to emerge sooner of later.

Preferably sooner. Travelling by Underground got right on her nerves.

'So what's it like, then?' she asked, as he counted the tickets for the second time. 'Being a servant of Sharon?'

'Charon,' he corrected tonelessly. 'I am a humble seeker who serves the dark ferryman to the best of my ability.'

'Ripping off travellers? You're too humble, you know. You're actually pretty good at it.'

'The security boys at the booth sighed and rolled their eyes heavenwards, as if asking forgiveness for this infidel's ignorance.

'The journey is a reflection of human life, sister. If you wish to make the journey, you must negotiate, and then pay, the appropriate price.'

Thinking about a woman falling out of a high building, many, many years ago, Jude murmured, 'Well, I can't disagree with you there.'

'Additional ticket thrown in, free and gratis,' he offered, lifting it to the light as if booking her, 'if you could spare a moment to discuss the doctrines of the Ferrymen of Eternity?'

'Sorry. In a hurry.'

'It's not true, you know,' he added conversationally, palming the extra ticket and handing her the agreed number. 'This rumour that we hypnotise people into joining us.'

'I'm sure it's not.' Jude tugged the tickets from his grasp. 'I'm sure you're the purveyors of genuine truth and wisdom, and we're all going to be sorry come Judgement Day. But I really have to be somewhere.'

'Loved one waiting?' the eyeless man asked, managing something distantly related to a benign smile.

'Yeah,' Jude admitted, pushing through the crudely-rigged turnstile towards the stationary elevators. 'And you wouldn't believe how long overdue I am.'

The southbound platform was near empty and even colder than she remembered. The overheads displays were working, though, alternating a probably optimistic arrival time for the next train with Ferryman slogans, which drew uneasy giggles from the lads arguing and posturing at the far end of the platform.

WHERE IS IT YOU'RE HEADED? the screen blared, silencing their laughter; THINK ON YOUR FINAL DESTINATION.

Good question.

She couldn't go to Fitch. Even if she (he? too many possibilities) still lived in the same house and worked in Club Andro, those would be the first places Warner would have staked out. She'd been too chatty, too careless all those years. Mentioned too many names, dropped too many hints. Between what she'd said directly to him, and what he could wring out of other employees, he could reconstruct practically her whole life.

This left her with two options. She could give herself up. Okay, let's give it due consideration. It wasn't like they were going to hurt her. She was the only ReTracer who'd ever travelled forward in time. She was a miracle. She was the most valuable thing on earth.

But valuable things got locked up for their own protection, and miracles existed solely for scientists to debunk or duplicate, preferably both. Right now, Jude trusted Warner and friends about far as she could thrown their damn techno-helicopter with one hand tied behind her back.

The alcohol she'd gulped at the canalside had settled her stomach, but her head felt like it was stuffed with feathers, heavy suffocated thoughts turning over and over in endless slow-motion. Fumbling in her pocket, she took the cap off the next miniature and drained it without thinking. Neat gin. Gin and despair in the ruins of the Underground, how Romantic.

Shit, she thought, I'm getting poetic. Things are definitely serious.

That leaves option two.

There's no guarantee that Warner won't trace you there. And you always said you'd never get that desperate.

She might not even take you in.

A low, bone-shaking rumble echoed up the unlit tunnel towards her. The other travellers – the boys wearing the red sash of the junior Sewer Rats, a courier hugging a suitcase to his chest, a couple of depressed-looking tarts in girlish floral dresses – gravitated slowly to the edge of the platform. Tense with the unfamiliarity of Underground etiquette, Jude hung back.

Hung back until the clanking mass of pistons and levers that passed for a steam engine had rattled to a halt, dragging the battered carriages level with the platform. Hung back until everyone was aboard, the boys yelping and bouncing on the threadbare seats. And then the engine was whining with a fresh head of steam and about to struggle onwards, and she had no choice but to take those last two steps towards the perpetually open doors and step aboard.

The tarts looked at her and sniffed, as if suspecting that she'd come to steal their customers. No one else seemed too interested. Most of the seats had been replaced with whatever came to hand; a plastic chair, a board, even a baby seat. The original, threadbare seats were the only ones occupied. Settling cautiously on a plank seat that immediately bruised her spine and filled her trousers with splinters, she realised why everyone else had been in such a hurry.

As she turned to scan the platform one more time, a final reassurance, a young man in a suspiciously expensive jacket hurtled from the stairwell. Tense, eager, and just a little too late. They were already moving, steam spiralling from the gap between the carriage and the track, obscuring his footing if he decided to jump.

'Hey, suit man!' one of the Sewer Rats yelled. 'Lost your limo?'

Her would-be tail broke stride, one hand moving inside his jacket. The taunting Sewer Rats ducked back behind the doorposts, squealing animal alarm-cries, as quick and wary as their namesakes.

In the next carriage, a long, lean figure stood up, flicking the dark silhouette of a weapon from his hip. Jude registered the tattoo on his neck. The shining eye of arcane knowledge, the mark of a Ferryman enforcer. Registering the movement, her tail frowned and slowly swung his empty hand away from his jacket. The enforcer bowed his head very slightly, acknowledging a professional courtesy, and turned to watch the grey-suited figure diminish as the tunnel raced forward to swallow them.

Suddenly, pathetically grateful for the Ferrymen's neurotic

anti-violence policy, Jude leaned back in her seat. A protruding stub of the original seat fitting connected with her elbow, adding another bruise to her collection.

'I hate travelling by Underground,' one of the tarts said, tugging listlessly at her stockings. 'The class of people you have to travel with, y' understand?'

Her companion glared meaningfully at Jude. 'Bloody gangs.'

'Bloody wage-slaves, more like. They cause all the real trouble. Gang boys, they're all right. Good customers. I was up Whitechapel the other day with one of the Barrier Boys, he bought me dinner and everything. Couldn't fault his manners. Those government types, they can't even manage a please and thank you.'

Jude fingered the material of her far-too-expensive jacket and wondered if she should stop off to go clothes shopping.

The connecting door jolted open and the tattooed enforcer swayed through it, lithely mirroring the movements of the accelerating carriage. He'd probably spent most of his adult life down here, riding the trains and dispensing lethal punishment to anyone who dishonoured the cult's 'sacred caverns'. No gang rivalries, no private quarrels, no violence verbal or physical, was tolerated below ground.

And annoying the enforcers was generally regarded as a pretty bad idea. Any of them who actually had to resort to violence to keep the peace were rendered ceremonially unclean by it, and had to undergo a complex forty-eight hour ritual before they could return to whatever bizarre form of worship took place on the platforms after dark. The slightest prospect of enduring that tended to make them rather annoyed.

Fixing her gaze on the garish slogans painted into the poster slots above her fellow passengers' heads, Jude sat very, very still.

'I must apologise for that small disturbance,' the enforcer said, retaining his balance perfectly as the carriage jolted across a damaged rail. 'It's always unfortunate when the karma of a journey is disturbed. Perhaps we might all share a moment of meditation, to restore the balance of our environment?'

By the time she changed lines at what remained of Green Park, the enforcer had the tarts sniffling sentimentally and crooning along with a mantra to the glory of Charon, and Jude was developing a headache.

The westbound train was in better repair, and quieter. Her seat was marginally more comfortable, and she spent the time pondering the slogans affixed over her fellow passengers' heads. LOOKING FOR A SIGN?, one said; WELL, THIS IS IT. And directly opposite, daubed in six-inch blood-red capitals: ETERNITY IS A LONG TIME TO THINK ABOUT WHAT YOU SHOULD HAVE DONE.

Yeah, preach it, brother.

Another enforcer got on at the first stop, strumming absently on a harp the size of a pizza and about as tuneful. A woman shepherding four or five children took over the end of the carriage, huddling on a broken car seat under a rambling slogan in Arabic. Jude amused herself for a couple more stops trying to count her brood, but they wouldn't stay still long enough. The carriage echoed to their voices, mostly monosyllabic cries of rage as they fought for toys or seats or their mother's attention.

It was only as the woman got up to leave that Jude thought she recognised her. The name was on her lips before she could stop herself.

'Yona?'

The woman looked round. Her hair hung lank, and she limped badly. It was hard to see the ghost of the giggly trainee ReTracer in her face, but it was there still, buried under years of resentment and despair.

'Well,' she said, as the children clustered around her, proving their allegiance in the face of this strange threat. 'Jude. You've obviously done well for yourself.'

For a moment, that made no sense; then she remembered the suit and the briefcase, and was about to protest, but Yona was already saying, 'I never thought you were the type.'

'You were right. I, er, should probably have left years ago.' Straining to put together the pieces, calculate how Yona's past might have been changed by this constant interference with reality, 'Like you did?'

'Oh yes,' Yona agreed, a death's-head grin spreading across her taunt face. 'Because that's the life, isn't it? Your only decision – today, do we beg, borrow, or steal?'

She nudged the oldest boy, a lanky thing of about ten, with big blue eyes and startlingly pale skin. Snapping into a familiar routine, he stepped forward and extended a hand in silent entreaty.

'What happened to you?' Jude asked his mother.

'Don't play dumb with me, Jude.' She was already shoving the youngest kids onto the platform; the carriage vibrated as the engine built up a head of steam for the next stage. 'We weren't all as lucky as you. Mart, c'mon!'

Confused by his role in this pageant of adult hostilities, the boy took a step back. Jude pressed the briefcase into his still outstretched hand, almost unbalancing him, and then he leapt from the moving train and was gone, hugging his unforeseen bounty as the cloud of steam in their wake blurred him into nothingness.

The enforcer frowned at her over his harp and began to play something that sounded unnervingly like a lament.

But he made no comment, the suitably elderly blind man at the barrier accepted her ticket without any attempt at evangelism, and she emerged on to the desolation of the Hammersmith flyover in the wake of a shower, the wet pavements glazed with sunlight.

Didn't look like Warner had anticipated this. No sign of helicopters, no sign of tails or armoured cars or any kind of official presence. Just the usual. Fires burning under the flyovers, kids rollerskating: racing each other, tag-teaming, hurling insults and stones across the central reservation to confuse the other team. Shabby men in leather coats hand-signalled the odds to one another, or counted gambled cash with the same mechanical precision as the blind ticket seller.

She wondered if the two worlds ever collided; if the touts would give odds on the arrival of the sweaty, reeking trains, or the Ferrymen had the faintest appreciation of the shouting, shrieking battles being fought in the world above.

We've separated off into our own little worlds. Legal or illegal, rich or poor, above the street or under it. Perhaps that's what the fortune teller in the park meant when she said the city was dying. It's not ceasing to exist, it's just changing. Fragmenting into ever smaller units, each isolated by an empty expanse of motorway or canal or abandoned parkland. A world of tribes lost in a concrete Amazon, each thinking themselves the sum of creation, blissfully unaware of what lies outside their little kingdom.

Jude ground her knuckles into her eyes, blinked a couple of times. Windows greased with rain reflected sunlight across the emptiness. Under the shadow of the high and glittering entrance of the Palais, a pack of scrawny dogs lounged, regarding her with suspicion. No doubt other eyes, human eyes, were watching too.

Hurrying despite the total, decades-long absence of traffic, she crossed the cracked expanse of the Broadway – a greenway now, tufted with grass and silvery thistles – into King Street.

The theatre was still standing. Which was good. In a manner of speaking. The sight of its cracked and patched glass frontage, the lopsided signs in the windows, sent a shiver through her. Unsure if it was terror or relief, Jude forced herself to keep walking. All the way up to the crumbling access ramp, the perpetually open door, and through into the gloom.

At what must have been the ticket desk, an old man was sitting with his feet on a wooden box, entering data via a keyboard with one crooked finger.

'Public meetings are Monday and Thursday,' he said gruffly, without raising his eyes from the screen. 'Please do take a leaflet.'

Jude shook her head. 'I'm here to see Ms DiMortimer.'

'On what business?'

'Call it a family reunion.'

'This is extremely tiresome of you, Judith,' the woman sprawled on the chaise lounge sighed as she entered. 'You know that I told everyone here that I don't have any children. What I'm going to say now, I really don't know.'

Jude stood there for a moment, watching the light of the candles on the window ledge play across her mother's face. It reminded her of the toy projector she'd had for her sixth birthday, a cheap rotating ball that scattered the bedroom ceiling with flecks of blue and gold. For the ten days until the batteries ran out. A light that seemed designed for hiding than for looking, for concealing things that neither of them wanted to face.

'That's nice,' she said.

'Oh, it's this damn stratification,' Milena DiMortimer sighed, sitting up with the lithe, balanced grace of a young girl. 'New revelations have proceeded from the Divine Link. No one gets to progress to Second Level Enlightenment unless all their close relatives are following the Path. Or dead.

Jude was about to blurt something stupid, something primal and hurt. Then she remembered that she was actually dead – legally dead anyway – and something else occurred to her.

'You don't seem surprised to see me.'

'Should I be?'

'Well. I – wondered if you'd had any calls from GenoBond.'

Drawing her perfectly manicured nails across her throat in a gesture of languid anger, Milena shook her head. 'Not for years. Not since they told me you were dead. Which was rather silly of them, since you're obviously not. You'd have thought they'd have learned to tell the difference by now. I'm just glad I didn't waste time going to the funeral.'

Advancing into the gloom, Jude looked around for somewhere to sit. Scraps of her past peeked at her from the rickety shelves, the folds of the ornate Indian rug hiding the stains on the sofa. No photographs, of course. Unlike the Ferrymen, the devotees of this religion left the entanglements of the flesh far behind them. Just ornaments, the familiar orange spine of a book, the blue and silver of a scarf she remembered her mother wearing to a school party. Secret memories, locked in everyday objects whose significance only the two of them could comprehend.

'I always had a suspicion,' Milena continued, 'that they'd turn out to be wrong about that. You always were an awkward child. Anything anyone ever told me about you was wrong. All your teachers, for a start. Didn't one of them say you were going to be in jail before you were fifteen? And remember that deacon who swore you were called to the priesthood?'

'He was a bishop. I think.'

'He was still wrong.'

Lowering herself cautiously onto the edge of the sofa, Jude asked softly, 'So. Mother. You are still taking the lithium?'

Milena froze. A split-second freeze to draw attention to her perfectly still hands before she adopted a comically shocked pose, all fingernails and pale lips. 'But of course I am, Judith dear. Can't you see the doctor waiting to sign my prescriptions? The dispensary in the foyer? The armoured car that ferries my drugs from the nearest Hurst three times a day?'

Sighing, Jude bowed her head.

I should never have come here. Too far apart, too much between us. But stubbornly, stupidly, I keep treading the same path in the hope that something will change. That some rote action or predictable response will suddenly turn under me like a loose stone and catapult me forward, into some new version of our relationship.

'I'm sorry for what they did,' she said, as she always did. 'Despite the fact that it wasn't my fault, I was a child and I couldn't stop them – I'm sorry for leaving you.'

Milena sighed.

'Now what?'

'I do wish you wouldn't keep bringing that up. Depressing thoughts do so lower the tone of the place. The spiritual atmosphere of the building really hasn't been up to scratch today. Probably the gulls.'

Jude couldn't quite suppress a frown.

'They gather on the roofs over there.' She waved a hand vaguely through the wall of the tiny room. 'They're all bugged, you know. We shot one once. Found a camera attached to the side of its head. That broke as soon as we touched it, of course. Specially designed to. They're clever like that. So we took the transmitter off its legs and sold it to one of the newspapers. They were really quite insulting about the whole business. The article described us as a colony of paranoid mental patients.'

Jude leant back into the uneven padding of the sofa. 'You are, Mum.'

'Paranoid?'

'Paranoid. Ex-mental patients. A colony. All correct so far.' The alcohol was adding an edge to her words that she'd never intended, and she was running out of energy. 'This was a mistake, wasn't it? I shouldn't have come. Or I should have come years ago, under different circumstances.'

Milena grunted. 'So. Go ahead.'

'What?'

'That's what you do, isn't it? Leap backwards through time to rescue the innocent.'

'It doesn't work like that. If it did, I would have gone back and stopped them from separating us. But apparently, being torn screaming from your only relative doesn't constitute a crisis, so no ReTracing permitted, so what's the point of the whole bloody thing anyway?'

Her mother looked at her and, just for a moment, she saw a flash of connection, of sanity, of real understanding even. Then Milena closed her eyes and the moment was gone, and to fill the silence Jude said 'Anyway, I can't do that any more.'

'Oh. Well. I doubt there was any future in it anyway. Did they show you the creation?'

'The what . . .?'

'The creation. My dear, you don't think we just lie here all day meditating and achieve nothing?'

Jude smiled what she hoped was an amused, endearing smile. She knew she just looked hostile. The mirror on the far wall told her that much. In this suit, she looked like an executive paying a sympathy call to a barely known colleague, guilty and shocked by what she'd found.

'Which is yet another reason why I can't have the lithium. The focus of the inner mind can only be achieved when the body is entirely free of pollutants. Apparently.' Milena stretched, sending a shimmer of movement through the tiny brass bells strung around her ankle. 'Pity, really. I do miss coffee.'

'There hasn't been real coffee on the streets for years.' Jude observed, thinking wistfully of Warner's office and his espresso machine, aluminium sticky with fingerprints.

'On your salary? You do surprise me. Don't the minions of the Government get whatever they want?'

'Mother. We agreed we weren't going to do this.'

'Do what?' Milena murmured, as wide-eyed as a child. 'Remind each other of our failings? Remind each other to take our respective poisons, like good meek little citizens?'

'You,' Jude said, unable to keep the smile from her face, 'were never a meek little citizen.'

'And still my little girl shifts history around for the Government.'

'Not any more, as it happens.'

'Hmmm,' Milena said, as if she doubted that. 'You still haven't looked at the creation.'

Waving a hand in acquiescence, Jude stood up. 'Where is it?'

'Outside.' A quick gesture toward the flaking rattan blind. 'Careful. Don't open it too far.'

Jude moved to the window, tugged lightly on the cord. Dust billowed from the folds as it furled, rising like a theatre curtain to reveal some unforseen wonder.

Whatever she'd been expecting, this was entirely . . . different.

Twisting, spiralling skyward on the vacant ground bordering the river, an anthill of rusted metal and moss rose slowly from the ruins. Pressing her face to the glass, she could distinguish the shapes of machinery, forklifts and strimmers and crane-arms, all subsumed into a Babel-tower twenty or thirty times the height of a man. Leaves poked from the crevices, tiny white flowers crowned jutting stumps or splayed like broken spider's webs from unfinished arms.

'What is it?'

'The beginning of a new city.'

Jude blinked, contempt choking on bewilderment. 'You're building this? But there's no scaffolding . . . How?'

Milena tapped the smooth skin of her temple with one long nail. 'Power of the mind.'

'Oh, for goodness sake.' Words failed her, and she stood for a time, watching the jagged silhouette shed dead leaves into the wind and thinking, If I saw it grow now, indisputably, what would I do? What would I believe?

'It's nice,' she said finally, turning away from the window. 'What's it for?'

Milena laughed.

'And that's funny because . . .?'

'If you have to ask, my dear, then there's no way I can explain it to you.'

'Platitudes. Great.' She stepped back, leaving the blind raised. 'So this is it. Ten years, and all you have to offer is a heap of rust and annoyance that I'm not dead.'

'And you, Judith? You haven't exactly been forthcoming. In fact,' shielding her eyes from the light, she managed a dry smile, 'you haven't been coming at all.'

'I have to go now,' Jude told her. 'My day's turning out to be pretty busy. It started pretty well, but now some time-travelling lunatics are trying to kill me – I think – and Warner wants to put me in a jar, and Fitch is a man, and frankly I don't know who you are. Guess I never did.'

Milena nodded. 'Let the blind down, dear. The sunlight burns me so.'

Releasing the cord, Jude watched the blind thump back into place. 'Better?'

'Oh yes. Now run along. Go do whatever it is you do as a cohort of the fascist repressors.' Closing her eyes, she relaxed back onto the curve of the chaise lounge and folded her hands dramatically across her chest. 'I have to finish the bracing section before Martina can work on the next level, and she'll only yowl about it all through dinner if it isn't ready on time. Take my advice, never get involved with redesigning reality. No one thanks you for it.'

Nodding confirmation of that particular, belated piece of wisdom, Jude turned her back on the tower of rust and walked away.

THIRTEEN

When she emerged into King Street, the rain was still falling.

Too tired to huddle or hunch or scurry, Jude tipped her head back and let the stinging, acrid droplets massage her face, smooth her wind-tangled hair. Nearby, a child was laughing behind a garden wall, a laugh of naughtiness and sheer delight at this peculiar adult. A smile tugged at the corners of Jude's mouth and, surprised, she gave way to it.

I'm wet, I'm catching cold, I've got nothing to my name but a handful of Underground tickets and a wallet full of debit cards I daren't use. My mother's every bit as mad as I expected – though it's hardly her fault – and more interested in psychic Lego bricks than in assisting her daughter to outrun the goon squad.

I'm out of places to go.

Water was pooling in her eyes, forcing her to blink, lower her head. She remembered crossing Tower Bridge in the rain, Fitch holding her hand like a child. A Sunday afternoon, and all the ships were in; lopsided planks and lurching, bobbing rope walkways down to the decks, where leather-faced Greens in from the hills would trade fresh vegetables and intricately carved bowls for knives or garden tools or salt. Fitch studying their grubby faces and ritual tatoos with such appalled astonishment that people started muttering about spies and 'Govimenters', and they beat a hasty retreat into the backstreets, looking for coffee and a culture that intersected more closely with their own.

I could go there. Get a ship owner to take me out of the city, round the coast. I've never been on a boat. Or hitchhike to a new city. Catch rides on the supply trains, flag down container trucks plying between Hursts. I've seen that on the TV, it doesn't look so hard.

There are a thousand places I could go, a million things I could do. All I have to do is put aside fate and predetermination and waiting for the right moment – and, for the first time in my adult life, decide.

Brilliance flickered across the puddles at her feet, reflected from some unseen corner of the sky. She thought it was lightening and turned, hoping for a sign, a direction, the hand of the Almighty inscribing her destiny in the sky.

All she saw was the searchlight beam skimming the wet tarmac of the Broadway like an accusing finger, backed by the steady chip-chop-chop of helicopter rotors.

Warner had picked a great time to come over all Sherlock Holmes, that was for sure.

'Jude!' the loudspeaker crackled, barely audible through the rotor noise and the rain. 'Let's be sensible about this.'

Jude simply stood there, watching the searchlight beam creep across the glistening road towards her as if hunting her out in the dark.

Too far to the dubious safety of the Underground. No point going back inside the theatre, either. It would take too long to galvanise the inmates to anything approaching resistance. Anyway, Warner's troops would eat that bunch of pathetic hippies for breakfast and still have an appetite.

Yet again, her options had been reduced to surrendering or running. She hated it when that happened.

But she ran anyway.

Back inside, but only to break their line of sight. The old man in the ticket booth looked up as she passed, puzzled, hands poised above the computer keyboard as if about to launch into a symphony.

'Are you here for the rent?' he asked.

'Well,' Jude growled, wrestling with the catch on the window beside him, 'I'm not here for the entertainment, that's for sure.'

The catch gave.

Vaulting the window ledge, she plunged feet-first through the narrow opening and down into the yard beyond. Car park, once upon a time. Still scarred by white lines and faded RESERVED FOR signs. Dead space, cluttered with tools, wheelbarrows with no wheels and the dead husks of container-grown trees. Open ground beyond, leading to the scorched and ruinous walls of former buildings, former shops and offices and homes, now indistinguishable piles of brick losing their outer layer of soot to the rain.

And there, beside the river, the corkscrew silhouette of the tower.

Hurling herself over the jagged wall shielding it from the main building, Jude made straight for it.

Instinct. Isn't it great, huh? Tells you to run upstairs when you're being chased, forgetting that, unlike woolly mammoths, bad guys can climb stairs. Tells you to seek cover when there's something in the sky, forgetting that helicopters have more patience than eagles and can hover, direct ground troops, and wait.

With instinct on their side, it was a wonder that the human race had been around so long.

The tower site reeked of rust. Rust, and something else; a sweet, tart smell, like lemons and honey. The smell of decay. Braces and buttresses reared like giant's feet all around her, guy cables plucked at her feet, threatening to trip her. Shying away from the overhang of the tower's foundations at the last moment, Jude swerved towards the more precarious shelter of a buttress jutting towards the river. Ducking under the long, low arch of metal, uncomfortably aware that she was wider than her cover in several places, Jude froze.

The rain had rallied for a final assault, blurring the air into a grey curtain. Helicopters buzzed, high and distant, like flies trapped behind glass. The leaves entwining the jagged tower fluttered in the wind, a ripple of perpetual motion. Now and then, their motion exposed a glimpse of some strange eco-system; white grubs burrowing, or a flicker of whiskers and eyes like amber beads.

And as she watched, pressed tight against the cold metal, the tower began to grow.

A milimetre, a few grains of rust; a tiny shifting and expansion that could be anything from rain damage to an optical illusion. Then a tiny spur of metal emerging from the rust, like a tendril feeling the way for the vine.

She jumped back, ducking into the shelter of a mangled car chassis part-transformed into a buttress. Damp patches flowered on her exposed shoulders. The thick material of her suit was becoming uncomfortably heavy, and she wasn't likely to win Best Dressed ReTracer any time soon.

She could hear the helicopter still, but not see it. Didn't matter. The moment it turned this way, they'd spot her, and she didn't fancy pressing any closer into this thing, not when it was actually, well, growing . . .

'Well,' she told the rain, 'I suppose I could always ReTrace.'

Actually, why not?

If she was Adrift – lost in time, wandering pointlessly from day to day of her existence – then she could simply move on to somewhere less dangerous. Whether she was dead or alive, it didn't –

The revelation hit her so hard she almost fell out into the rain.

She wasn't dead.

If this was the year 32 After Migration and she was alive here, she had a body here to travel forward into, then she couldn't have died in 27 A.M., either by bullet or defenestration. A fact so simply, blindingly obvious that she'd managed to completely ignore it.

None of which explained what had actually happened here, or how to put it right, but at least she wasn't going to wake up in '27 trapped in a rotting corpse, or anything equally Gothic and impossible.

She fumbled in her pocket, found another of the miniatures looted from the hotel mini-bar. Scotch. That was more like it. She gulped the contents, coughing as the liquid bathed the back of her throat in ethanol and fumes.

Use your head for once and not your feet. Think.

All she needed to do was relax. Convince herself that she'd done whatever she needed to do here, and whatever arcane part of her mind controlled these things would boomerang her back into time. Or forward, for all she knew. The important thing was – away from here.

Grinning like a kid, Jude peered out from her precarious cover. Yeah, the ruin of that house looked pretty stable. Hop over the back wall there, nice and easy, and she could stroll right out through the front door to meet them.

GenoBond's finest, Gawd bless 'em, were busy staking out the area – a shabby shopping street scattered with burnt-out cars and fractured saplings – and for a moment they didn't even notice her.

There she was, strolling down the uneven pavement with her hands in the air, while, five dozen teenagers in smart green uniforms scuttled here and there, shouting orders, toting flash-stunners and totally ignoring her.

She felt pretty stupid. More importantly, considering the high lunatic quotient that had suddenly appeared when she'd come face to face with Warner at the canalside, she felt lethally exposed.

I should yell. Or maybe I shouldn't. They all look pretty

trigger-happy. I should have picked up a white flag on my way out. From somewhere. They're always conveniently to hand in the movies.

Maybe I'll just keep on walking.

Then one of the mini-tank drivers saw her and started yelling, and within three seconds she was walking towards a wall of taut faces and levelled guns.

'Hey, Warner! Isn't it about time you trained these pretty boys properly?'

The helicopter's tail swung rakishly around as it dipped, heading for the blank tarmac of the road ahead of her. The way the pilot was throwing it around, he was either grossly incompetent, or thought he was a Navy combat ace. The two might very well be connected. The loudspeaker was growling some counter-insult, but Jude elected to ignore it.

Several women in the saffron-yellow robes of the Devout Brides Of The Messiah were leaning out of the upper window of an old carpet shop, nudging one another and giggling. She couldn't hear exactly what they were saying, but judging from the interesting shade of crimson that the nearest troops were turning, it was the usual offer of heavenly bliss by way of certain earthly delights.

At least that broke the tension. The gun muzzles were lowered, the tanks stopped at a respectful distance. Up and down the street, raised curtains fell back into place as the residents lost interest. Just another average day in Hammersmith.

As she drew level with the carpet shop and the sniggering Brides, two troopers met her in the middle of the street and frisked her. They didn't exactly look happy about that part. The state her suit was in by now, she didn't blame them.

The helicopter was down, the rotor noise slowing, fading. The door slammed and she heard Warner's voice, tight with strain. 'Stand down. The prisoner goes in the truck – the rest of you, load up and meet us back at base. Come on, let's move it!'

He was already headed for the truck, a battered prison van with barred windows and a forest of aerials and comms dishes on the roof. Jude watched his retreating back. He looked thinner. And older. No, not older, she decided, as he hunched his shoulders to confront the driving rain. Old. Just old.

The muscle-boys nudged her forward and she obeyed. Docile, letting them steer her towards the open rear door. That last jolt of alcohol had found its way into her system, and she felt hot and dizzy and weak. By the time they reached the truck, her knees were buckled and the troopers had to haul her bodily into the back.

'Hello there, boss. Have you come to hand over my five years' back pay?'

Warner wrinkled his nose at her. 'You smell like a dead rat in a brewery waste bin. There are clean clothes in the corner, and a washcloth. Do something about yourself.'

'People have been saying that to me for years,' Jude muttered, mostly from habit.

The jumpsuit looked prison issue, but she wasn't feeling fussy. They'd left a bottle of water on one of the plastic bucket-seats, too. Ripping the cap off, she upended it over her head, splattering the thin carpeting with icy water. Grime and semi-dissolved acids flowed in long streaks down her forehead, stinging her lips.

Warner grunted, turned his attention to the muscle-boys. 'You can ride up front. She's not going to give me any trouble.'

'You sure about that?'

'You're in no fit state to give anyone any trouble, Jude. Just sit down and clean yourself up.'

The doors slammed closed. An internal lock thumped into

place: an external bolt, then another. They weren't taking any chances.

Stripping off the suit, she became aware of dry warmth circulating from under the seats, laced with the scent of petrol. They hadn't bothered to provide her with any shoes, which said something about their intentions. They weren't planning on her walking out of here any time soon.

Warner sat down. 'So why did you surrender?'

'I just remembered. I haven't had my Christmas bonus.'

Even with her back turned, she could feel his smile. 'For which year?'

'I always liked you, Warner,' she announced, muffled under a turban of towelling. 'Did I ever mention that?'

'Only when drunk.' Warner turned in his chair, folding both hands behind his head in a half-hearted stretching motion. 'Well, here we are at last. What's that poem? "Stone walls do not a prison make, nor iron bars a cage."?'

Jude, wriggling hurriedly into the jumpsuit before he got any ideas, only grunted.

'Particularly, the poet might have observed, if one is a ReTracer.'

Sounds like he'd guessed her masterplan.

'Unless, of course, he has some of this.'

When she turned, he was standing beside a cabinet set into the padded wall, a loaded syringe in his hand.

'All right, Warner,' she said softly, watching the glitter of striplight on the needle with the fascination of a cornered animal, 'what's the dope for?'

'For stopping a ReTracer from, well, ReTracing.'

Problem. Big problem.

Jude sat down, hoping the gesture would lull him into a false sense of security. Okay, grip the edges of the seat, tense the leg muscles ready to kick . . .

But Warner was moving away, back out of reach, the syringe held negligently at his side.

'We could hold you as long as we need to,' he reminded her, tapping the syringe against his thigh. 'To ask questions. Do the usual tests. Find out how this happened. And how to duplicate it. Publish a paper. Publish a book. I could get a Presidential Commendation, a medal, a seat on the board. You get the general idea.'

Poised to resist, and yet knowing that she wouldn't have to, Jude watched.

'Or . . .' Warner looked down at the syringe.

'Or . . . ?'

For answer, he turned on his heel, stabbed the needle into the grey wadding lining the walls and depressed the plunger.

Jude blinked.

'You got old, Warner,' she said finally, watching the pulse beating at his temple. 'Ran out of ambition. Lost your nerve.'

'I lost my taste for some of the shite that's been happening recently, that's for sure.'

She busied herself unwrapping the towel from her head, combing her wet hair back with her fingers. Right. Feeling better. Fully dressed, warm, comfortable. Even relatively clean. All I have to do is relax, and I can be out of here before Warner has time for a change of heart.

Relax, right. Easier said than done.

'And what kinds of things would those be?'

Warner sat down again, just across the van from her. Their knees were almost touching. 'The thing is, Jude I have this one last little job for you.'

'Aren't there laws against hiring the dead?'

He almost smiled.

'I want you,' he said, 'to go back to Year Zero and make sure no ReTracer prevents bioteching from being legalised, or invented, or however they're going to tackle it. I want you to stop them changing the future.'

Words failed her.

'I checked your records, Jude. Even back in 27, you'd heard the rumours. You knew GenoBond, and our elected masters, wanted bioteching either controllable, or non-existent.'

Jude pressed her fists against her temples, trying to squeeze some kind of lucidity back into her pummelled brain. 'That was Harchak, damn it. He was paranoid. Ninety-nine percent of everything he said to me was crap.'

'It's the other one percent you should be worried about. And Harchak has good reason to distrust GenoBond. They've cheated him before, they'll do it again without a second thought.' He seized her damp hand, held it for a moment. 'Think about it. You were there to hear that rumour, and you're here now, the only one who's able to stop them. That's not coincidence.'

'No, it's not. It's all part of me trying to stop myself falling out of a window. This – even this impossible jaunt into the future, breaking every rule of ReTracery – is all part of my attempt to save myself.'

I really have to find another way to solve my problems.

She was laughing. High, thin laughter that didn't sound like her at all. 'No,' she stammered, fighting her own alcohol-numbed senses. 'This is ridiculous. I'm not some kind of time-travelling hero. How am I going to stop anyone doing anything? Besides. How would they get back that far? It's impossible.'

'They have three top level ReTracers. People who've been able to travel through time without limitations, like you do now, for years. Sometimes naturally, sometimes with a little re-engineering. You found out about DiFlorian, but I suppose you never realised why they were working on her . . .'

DiFlorian. Well, that explains why I was never meant to find out what really happened to her. I was the dupe, supposed to walk in, make routine enquiries, report that everything was in order. But I was already ReTraced and looking for answers of my own, and I found out things I was never supposed to even guess at.

'We call them Travellers,' Warner was saying. 'They're due to ReTrace to Year Zero in a couple of hours. That's why you've ended up here. You're being drawn to them.'

'Because I'm one of them.'

Oh boy. That actually makes sense. The fortune-teller in the park mentioned Year Zero. If they didn't want me to know what they could do – what I could do – that would have been enough to get her killed. And Schrader, in the Hurst. Vanishing into thin air.

I do hate it when Warner's right. It goes against the natural order of things, your boss being right.

'All right. Let's say I believe this. Just for the sake of argument. First problem: I can't control where and when I ReTrace to. It's involuntary, instinctive. I can't just select Year Zero and off I go.'

'Travellers can.'

Ah. Good point.

'Anyway. You don't need to.' Warner fixed her with an icy stare. 'Stopping them is the key to your current problem. So, now you have all the facts, as soon as you ReTrace, you'll end up in the right time and place.'

'Yeah, I've heard that before. And how can you know what the key to my problem is when even I don't know?'

Warner sighed. 'I'm sorry to have to break it to you like this, Jude,' he said, soft and clear as a father with a dying child. 'But stopping the Travellers is definitely the answer to your problem. Because, when they realised that you could stop them – that you were the only person who could – they ReTraced to the year '27, and at 2.43 in the afternoon, they threw you out of a ninety-first storey window. It took the police four hours to scrape you off the pavement.'

Glancing down, Jude realised that she'd dug her nails into her palms until they drew blood.

'They killed me. Schrader and his buddies – he's one of them, isn't he? I mean – I did actually die?'

'I'm so sorry. There was nothing I could do. All the official channels were closed, everyone I approached had their orders and their excuses ready to hand. I've spent years trying to work out how to get a message back to you, find a way to warn you.'

'I'm dead.' The padded space blurred strangely, her cheeks stung; Jude realised abruptly that she was crying. 'My God, what must Fitch think?'

Hands closed around her wrists. Warner was kneeling in front of her, staring up into her face, cool and stern. 'Jude. Listen to me. You're not dead. Not really. Because you're here. As long as you're still ReTracing from that day, looking to find a way to reverse things, your death hasn't happened yet. You're outside time. Alive. And you can stop them.'

Jude held her breath until her vision swam red, then exhaled. She felt tired, ragged and not a little stupid. 'Right. I get it. But I still have one question. Why do I have this feeling that you're not doing this out of the kindness of your heart?'

He shrugged. 'I don't think that messing with history is a good –'

'Then you've been in the wrong job for twenty years. Come on, let's have the truth. What's in it for you, Warner?'

'Remember Andrew Marcus?'

Jude frowned with the effort. 'Your son. Yeah. I suppose.'

'Miserable kid, wasn't he?'

'I don't really –'

'Delicate. Bookish. Clingy. And those are the good points.'

Jude leant back in the chair, closed her eyes. 'Let me guess.'

'I now have a daughter named Andrea May. And she's happy. Biotech has changed all our lives – and what's wrong with that?' Warner touched her shoulder lightly; opening her eyes, Jude felt obliged to meet his gaze. 'Go and stop them, Jude. For her. For all of us.'

'Oh, cut the politicking crap, Warner. I don't have any choice and you know it. If I stay here, I'm a lab rat for Geno-Bond. If I do manage to ReTrace to another part of my life, I have nowhere to settle, no one to go to. And now these Travellers of yours know I'm still around, and I'm a threat to them, they'll track me down, right?'

'I would imagine so.'

'But I want you to know that you're a liar, a traitor and an accessory to illegal and treasonous activities, and I'm not doing it for you.'

His jaw tightened, just a little, and he stood up. 'I don't give a shit who you do it for, Jude. Just as long as you do it.'

Year Zero. This is nuts. I wasn't even born then. I'll probably get lost – or arrested as a lunatic or something.

'Got a sedative in that medical kit?'

'But of course.'

Jude rolled up her sleeve.

As the needle went in, she thought back to the Hurst, and Schrader, fading like a good memory the morning after. 'So, when I ReTrace, will I disappear, like Schrader did? Completely?'

'I'm not sure,' Warner admitted, depressing the plunger. 'I've never actually seen them in action. Why don't you pop back, after you've finished the job, and I'll buy you coffee and tell you all about it?'

FOURTEEN

Year Zero

Bang.

For a moment, Jude thought she'd run out of time and hit ground, future/present/now. Expected to feel herself bleeding, slipping, falling away for good into whatever not-darkness lay beyond.

Then the sound came back on. Caught up with her, snap, like someone had leant on the mute button. And there was noise. Traffic, voices, music, hurry-bustle-chatter-desperation-noise.

Jude was face down on the pavement, too winded to cry out, one arm trapped under her, and people were stepping right over her.

To be fair, they had to. There was no room on the pavement to step round. Wall to gutter people, shoving, squirming, pushing, clinging to a partner's arm as if afraid to lose them. Children squeezed between their feet. Dogs squeezed between the children.

It was like the worst ever fire evacuation from Club Andro – the one where every single customer seemed to be doped and couldn't tell the fire exits from the wall paintings – but with purpose. Going places, and fast.

What the hell was happening?

To her right, a glimpse of the wall, and safety. She took it. Concertinaed to her feet like a gymnast and leapt for it, screaming.

People got out of her way. The look on her face, they'd have been stupid not to.

A moment's deep breathing, sweaty palms pressed to the cold metal of locked security shutters, and Jude felt ready to lift her gaze from the few precious inches of empty pavement between her feet, and take a look at the street.

Solid with people. Faces at all the windows, on the doorsteps, huddled on the traffic islands. All the way to the blinking stop-go lights and the snail's crawl of cars, glistening from recent rain. Attack of the Sardine People.

And most of them didn't smell so good, either.

Crowds were one thing; but the noise, the cars, the way the air hung heavy around her, thick with other people's sweat? The sheer pressure of being hemmed in by buildings full to the brim with people, and people's things, and the things people were about to buy and make and consume? There was no way she could cope with this.

And then she remembered. The heat, the exhaust haze, the smell of random, entangled perfumes. Being carried on her mother's shoulders though a crowd so deep that she couldn't see the other side, leaning down to listen to murmured reassurances: 'Just a couple more shops now, Jude, and we can go home.'

It really was like this, before the Migration.

'All right?'

An old woman, leaning in to frown at her. Too close: close enough to smell her hair lacquer, see the red veins of her eyes, an unimaginable invasion of space outside a club or an extremely intimate relationship.

Wrinkled fingers poked her in the shoulder, hard enough to hurt. 'I said, are you all right?'

Resisting the urge to shrink back into the shutters, Jude managed a nod. 'Fine. I just – fell. I'm fine. Thanks.'

The woman nodded, as if she was relieved not to have to get any further involved, and slotted herself back into the contraflow of the crowd. Within seconds, she was gone;

another perfectly fitting piece in the ever moving puzzle, another drop in the ocean.

Jude exhaled.

This wasn't going to be a pleasant trip.

For a start, just look at these people. Oh yes, there were some ugly bastards working for GenoBond. No gene jobs, no quick fixes for them, with their talent hanging in the balance every time someone stirred up their DNA. Some had the free plastic surgery the company offered – though more for self-preservation than aesthetics. People who looked like that and didn't do something about it were obviously anti-bioteching Luddites, and in most areas of the city, Luddites were only safe while carrying serious armaments.

Even if they didn't have the surgery, most people in her time were born of variously 'perfect' parents, inheriting whatever genetic fixes they'd had. None of them looked like this.

Scowling, limping, hunching, hobbling and crawling. Sick. Old. Anorexic with self-disgust, swollen with self-pity. Unrefined, random and different.

And there were millions of them.

Pressing her back against the metal, reminding herself that she was safe from one direction at least, Jude spent a while just concentrating on breathing. Standing here, that was fine. That was manageable. And if she got desperate enough, she could always climb the drainpipe, hopefully there weren't laws against that . . .

Year Zero. Yeah, great idea.

As soon as she caught up with Warner again, she was going to break his immaculately re-gened nose. Of course, he wouldn't know why, because things would be dealt with, the loop would be closed, he would never have met her in '32 and told her to do any of this. She'd probably get fired.

Yes, that was definitely going on her 'to do' list.

She shrugged, trying to shift the weight of her heavy jacket. Leather. Probably real leather, too. That was vile. Plain top, jeans, running shoes. Pretty much what the downmarket end of the crowd were wearing. Some things hadn't changed much in the last few decades.

This looks like my body – but I wasn't even born in this year. Did I create it as I arrived? Bringing it back with me from '32? How?

You could definitely go crazy thinking about all this.

A child's arm lashed out, catching her across the knee. A boy in ugly trousers, one arm locked in his mother's death-grip, the other flailing in wild aggression at anyone within reach. Jude understood exactly how he felt.

Sooner or later, she was going to have to move from here.

What was it they said in school, about the time the Migration started? That urban overcrowding caused aggression, and the only way people could cope with it was to ignore each other, dehumanise each other, treat people the same way as the lampposts and litter bins. And that, of course, led to all kinds of problems. Crime and aggression and lack of social skills, all the way down to mass murder and dropping litter. So they'd said. 'Of course, it'll all be different out in the Hursts . . .'

Treat people as fixtures and fittings. Fine. She could do that.

That bastard Schrader did it all the time.

Trying to disguise her trembling as an occasional shiver of cold, Jude took a sidestep into the crowd, and somehow made it all the way to the curb without screaming.

It was quite easy, once you got the hang of it. She let the crowd carry her around for a while. Cushioned by a ring of arms folded, eyes-averted people, even crossing the road was easy. Green light or not, any car faced with that amount of mass was going to let it through.

She even knew where she was. Up on the northern edge of the main commercial area. Shop signs, brighter than she remembered, drew her in, a moth to a half-familiar flame. Dark windows crammed with dusty salvage had given way to sparse and brilliantly illuminated displays of pristine boxed electronics. Most of the contents would be back here, displayed in the same windows, in her time, hawked for a few coins or for barter.

These were even the same people. Tourists and time-wasters, the rich and the under-employed. Kids skipping school; an easier proposition in her time than in this, from the furtive way they watched any uniform appearing in the crowd. Teenagers, lacking all sense of urgency, squandering money and time with equal abandon. All the same types, just multiplied a hundred-fold.

The pub they'd raided to furnish the house for Fitch was just round the corner. She ought to go round and check out the decor. See if the bead curtains were up yet. They'd certainly looked old enough.

Someone jogged her arm, startling her, and she decided it was time for a rest. Lean into the crowd, turning yourself to signal which way you were going. Use your hands if you have to, but subtly. Casual gestures that just happened to have the effect of moving people aside. Some people gave way, others didn't. But that was all right. You moved in stages, taking whatever room you were given. Keeping your arms folded in to keep other people's hands out of your pockets – and to keep everyone else that little bit further away. Keeping yourself safe.

Switching streams to turn right, towards some kind of park entrance, Jude thought, this Living Before The Migration business, it's not so bad once you get the hang of it.

The park turned out to be a false alarm. Some kind of garden, yes. And pretty. But the gates were marked PRIVATE and padlocked. Given that there didn't even seem to be anyone in there, what was the point of that?

She positioned herself with her back to the gates – careful not to hide the PRIVATE sign, which was keeping a three-foot clear zone round her – and considered her options.

Going to the authorities was definitely out. Anyway, they might not know any more than she did. Biotech probably wasn't even public yet. No, she was going to have to sort this out on her own.

So, yes, Mr Warner, I just strolled into the lab as these all-powerful Travellers of yours were about to destroy the first successful regening experiments, and I simply overpowered them with the force of my personality. All in a day's work for Jude DiMortimer, super-Traveller.

The lab.

That was another thing. She was going to have to work out where they were.

She must have ReTraced to somewhere in the right area. That was how things worked. And Warner said she was being drawn through time to these Travellers anyway. So, somewhere round here.

And somewhere small. Maybe not officially a lab at all. Bioteching had been perfected during some kind of crack-down, hadn't it? An attempt to regulate genetic experimentation after some kind of over-hyped disaster. The law-makers cracked down on everything – and 'everything' went underground, took stupid, unregulated risks, and made the traditional giant leap for mankind.

What had the first companies been called? So many, now the tech had been licensed, pirated, extorted and stolen. BodyTech, BioDiverse, geneClean . . . All too obvious. During a crackdown, they'd have been called something neutral, something that might pass for a computer company or a standard medical research outfit.

Century Technology. They'd had a place on Great Windmill Street, a whole block, back before the Migration had leeched all the big players from the city and left the field to backstreeters like Harchak. Now, if they'd started off in that location, and expanded . . .

It was as near to useful information as she was likely to get. And anyway, this was ReTracing. Her problem didn't really need to be hunted down. All she needed to do was keep busy until it came up and slapped her in the face.

Then someone spoke her name and she looked up, timestreams colliding in her head. Overlaying the blonde woman's dreary department-store raincoat with the memory of a silk overcoat and patent shoes, her frown with the smile of a killer.

Little Miss Leather Shoes And Matching Handbag, who'd tried to kill her on the SideRide in Little East Bankside, and succeeded in a tastefully decayed backstreet twenty years later.

Or not. It was getting a little hard to tell.

'Well,' Jude said, because it was the only thing that came to mind that wasn't childishly obscene. 'Fancy seeing you here.'

'The place to be,' Little Miss agreed, 'if you're a sardine.'

'Or a homicidal maniac.'

'Now, Jude, that's no way to talk about yourself.'

'Wow, you're a natural, Miss Prim. Do they have Friday Night Comedy Showcase in this century?'

The pressure of the crowd was pushing them together, nudging her nemesis towards the rear of the pavement. The blonde woman spread her empty hands and smiled. 'All right, let's take the wisecracking as read and get down to the talking.'

She's scared of me.

'Talk, right. Like you did last time we met?'

She just kept on smiling. 'That's all over, Jude. I can't hurt you now. Not like that, anyway.'

'Because I'm dead.'

'Because you're like us. The dying – or the continual ReTracing, something – pushed you over the edge. Awakened your latent abilities. I could stick a knife in you right now, and you'd be gone before it touched you. You're no longer tied to your body – and that makes you indestructible.'

'Thanks for the tip.'

Little Miss frowned. 'You don't believe me.'

'I don't believe anyone hands the advantage to their enemy by telling them they're the Woman of Steel.'

The blonde woman glanced away. Just for an instant, and without her gaze seeming to settle anywhere, but Jude marked the direction anyway and began circling against the slow current of bystanders, to check it out.

'The fact is,' the woman said wearily, 'I'm not your enemy. Why don't we go somewhere less crowded? There's a square this way – without the padlocks . . .

'No.' Jude nodded in the opposite direction. Away from whatever Little Miss was so interested in, off in the crowd. 'That way. Walk.'

'It's too busy to –'

'That way, or nothing.'

Shrugging annoyance, Little Miss started to walk.

By the next intersection, Jude knew the street by name. Collymore Street, leading down into a jumble of theatres, takeways and clubs that still existed, much diminished, in her day. Shapeless blocks of concrete and glass jutted over a narrow road choked with erratically parked cars, offering unpredictable impediments to the speed-crazed cyclists.

The crowds had thinned, but there were still enough bystanders around to make her nervous. People in bad suits smoking in doorways, or grunting and twittering into mobile phones, raising their gaze to the thin ribbon of blue sky now and then, as if in desperation.

She glanced back down the street. It didn't look like they were being followed, but since she didn't have much idea who the third Traveller was, it was impossible to be sure. Any of these office boys or lost tourists could turn on her any second.

With what weapons, Jude? You don't even exist here.

Lunging forward, Jude grabbed the woman by the shoulder and swung her round; fast, hard, stopping her with the heel of her hand on the other shoulder. Looked dramatic, and probably felt it, too. The two lads sharing a cigarette on the steps a few doors away looked up, blank as corpses. Probably wondering if they were about to witness some of that inner-city crime they were always hearing about on the news.

Little Miss Prim wasn't looking happy. But, despite the obvious shape of an underarm holster showing through the immaculate cut of her jacket, she hadn't gone for a weapon.

So maybe it was true. They couldn't hurt her any more.

Riding her new-found confidence, Jude leant forward, deliberately invading her personal space, and snapped, 'The other Travellers. Where are they?'

'And why would I want to tell you that?'

'Because I'm more powerful than any of you, shit-for-brains. I'm dead – and still moving through time. I have the power to twist time any way I want, and if I decide to throw you down the bottomless pit of eternity, there's no way you can stop me.'

To her surprise, she sounded pretty convincing. And Little Miss looked faintly worried.

Good. It looked like these Travellers were only half a step ahead of her in the theory department, and weren't entirely sure where she fitted in to the scheme of things. She could use that.

'I can't tell you where they are,' the blonde woman said, 'because I don't know. They arrived separately. Could be anywhere.'

Jude leant closer, clasping her shoulder with one hand, lowering her voice to a growl. 'So take me to where you're going to meet them.'

'All right. Fine. But we have half an hour, so it won't hurt for you to give me a chance to explain, now will it?'

'Explain what? How you're so sorry you tried to kill me – whoops, I mean "actually did kill me", don't I?'

Miss Handbag sighed. 'I did what I had to do. I'm not saying I'm proud of that – but it looks to me like you're on the "by any means necessary" trail yourself, so maybe you should climb off your high horse for a moment.'

'I'm not –'

'A killer? Sure. So how are you planning to stop us from trashing Century Tech and bombing Martin H.'s few remaining brain cells back to the stone age?'

The surprise must have shown on her face, because Little Miss was fighting a smile. 'Nice to see you were well briefed. Who did send you after us, anyway? Njallsson? Warner doesn't have the guts. Kelly Kotomo, of course. A conspiracy among you street-kids-made-good, that would really appeal to you, wouldn't it?'

'What appeals to me right now,' Jude muttered, 'is shoving you in front of the next moving vehicle I see. Unfortunately, this seems to be a quiet street. So state your case, fast, before one comes along.'

Adjusting the weight of the bag on her shoulder, she fixed Jude with a cold stare. 'It's simple. We're going to win. You can't stop us. You have exactly one choice – you can be on the winning side, or the losing one. It's up to you.'

Jude drew breath, fighting the unfamiliar tang of carbon and sweat that seemed to be choking her. 'Will you really be that surprised if I say – no deal?'

A long wail of sirens; coloured lights flickered as a police car raced through the parallel street. Despite herself, Jude glanced back, a reflex born of long nights of mischief on the Bankside that hadn't even happened yet.

Little Miss ducked out from under her hand, turned on one stiletto heel, and bolted.

This, Jude thought, starting after her, is where I'm going to wish I'd kept up that gym membership Fitch bought me.

No problem. I can do this. I'm better dressed for running than she is. Woah, watch the car . . . Look at her, can hardly walk in those shoes, let alone run. Turning left now – if she doesn't fall over that stray toddler first.

Another backstreet, bins and fire escapes. Go on, give in to instinct, run upwards and trap yourself –

All right, then, don't. Still gonna catch you. Thanks to the running shoes. I wonder how Warner arranged that? Or perhaps I did. Perhaps there's a part of me that foresees how I need to be dressed, and arranges . . .

Shit. Now where's she going?

A recessed doorway in the alley wall, a glimpse of a bulky figure leaning out to shepherd her inside.

A safe house.

She arranged this. Suggested we walked one way, knowing I'd choose the other. Towards her escape route, her back-up, just in case the attempt to win me over didn't work.

And she's gone.

Skidding to a halt three paces from the door, Jude drew herself up to her full height. That left her only about eight inches shorter than the bruiser currently occupying the whole doorway.

Then she saw the gold letters on the plaque half-hidden by his elbow, and realised exactly how well prepared her adversaries were.

'Stand aside,' she snapped, 'on the authority of the Department of GenoBonded Psi-Talent Operatives.'

His eyes narrowed, just a little, and she knew exactly what was passing through his head. Where does she know that name from?

The real question, big fella, is – how come you recognise it, years before GenoBond was founded?

Perhaps because its initials are embossed on the doorbell plaque right beside you?

'I'm sorry,' he said mildly, steadying himself to repulse an expected attack. 'This is a private club. Members only.'

'Okay, fine. And what do you think the police are going to say when I report all this to them?'

The bruiser raised an eyebrow, an attempt at subtlety that sat uneasily on his big, blank face. 'I daresay, madam, that they'll agree that private clubs are perfectly legal. If you'd like to apply for membership, I'll be happy to take your details, but the waiting list is rather lengthy.'

'Forget it,' Jude murmured, turning away. 'I'll just . . .'

It had been a long time since her last kick-boxing lesson. In fact, the last person she'd used it on had been Lazy Jay. Her reflexes were rusty, but the big guy wasn't likely to be quick on his feet, so –

Swiveling on one foot, Jude planted the other solidly into the bruiser's lower stomach.

He didn't move a muscle.

'. . . go,' Jude conceded, withdrawing from the awkward stance with what little dignity she could muster. 'I'll just go.'

The bruiser bowed his head slightly, infinitely polite. 'I think that would be wise, madam.'

End of the alley: an open square, crowded with sweaty men eating ice cream, screaming kids, a few ragged women staking out the benches with carrier bags stuffed with litter. End of the alley, end of the line.

I wonder what Little Miss Handbag would have done if I'd said yes?

If they really can't harm me, if I am dead to the physical world, they'll be desperate to find another way to stop me. Buy me off. Win me over. Something.

Otherwise, this could go on forever. Me chasing them through time, always patching up the damage they've done. Them just about to wrench history round to the way they want it, only for me to head them off at the pass – again.

The novelty of that could wear off real fast.

I'm going to have to find some way to stop them. Permanently. And preferably, this trip. I've had enough of all this. ReTracing. GenoBond. Everything. It turns out there really is no place like home.

A car nudged its way round the perimeter of the square, clearing a path through a group of giggling office girls headed for the withered lawns, clutching brown paper bags and drinks bottles wet with condensation. Suddenly, giddyingly, she was aware of the whole city writhing around her, a mass of her ancestors pacing familiar paths, enacting comfortable rituals, oblivious to the battle being fought right under their noses.

Century Technology. Well, at least I know where they're going to turn up.

Darting between parked vehicles, Jude emerged into the sunlight.

It would have been nice, she was beginning to think, to have lived here before. When the city was full to bursting. Irritating, all these people, and the sweat-perfume smell made her skin crawl. But still. There was something about it all. The continual background noise, where her city had a dappled pattern of sound and silence, every street pulsing to a different rhythm. The colours, the ever-shifting window displays and the vibrant poster boards. The voices, raised in laughter without fear of what kind of attention they might attract.

Very strange, and beautiful.

Turning at the corner of Great Windmill Street, she glanced back at the cars and the tourists and the children waiting for things they didn't need or appreciate, and thought: I need a soapbox.

Woe unto you, great city, for the end is nigh. Another three decades and there'll be wolves scavenging in this street.

Actually, that was partially my fault – but the animals had just been abandoned after the last zoo keeper walked out, it was cruel, we were only going to let the herbivores out but we were drunk, made a little mistake with the cages . . .

Another three decades and ninety-nine out of every hundred of you will be gone. Fled to the Hursts, or dead in the gang wars. And who'll be left? You, the child with the ice-cream, tired and old and hustling for a living? You, with your shabby carrier bags leaking your few belongings as you walk? You, suit man, tending lettuces on a bomb site in Whitechapel, the nine-to-five forgotten and unmourned?

Parasites on a decaying corpse of a place. Wolves and gangs and the Ferrymen and Club Andro and me, all trying to get on with our lives.

At the next corner, where the vast skyscraper housing Century Technology's immaculate consultation rooms and tasteful display labs should have stood, there was a music shop.

A low little shop, with a crooked doorframe and wide first-floor windows cluttered with dead plants and stacked paperwork. A dormer window in the roof was leaking the stop-start sound of someone practising the saxophone. Badly.

She stopped at the low, dangerously spiked railings surrounding the basement access, and stared at the gleaming brass instruments ranged in the main window, stunned by unexpected defeat.

Now what?

Downstairs, behind the blacked-out windows of the basement, she caught the sound of breaking glass.

Bracing herself carefully on the few sections of railing that weren't razor sharp, Jude leaned over to read the metal doorplate.

CENTURY TECHNOLOGY. PLEASE RING FOR ATTENTION.

FIFTEEN

She rang the bell four times before there was any sign of life from within. That gave her more than long enough to notice the flaking paintwork, the weeds scraping an existence between the flagstones, and realise that this wasn't exactly a high class operation.

But that didn't surprise her, not really. A lot of things, from music to computers, had started in back alleys and basements. Big companies had never had much time for research. It was easier to wait for some obsessive working from his parents' garden shed to make the breakthrough, and then buy it off him.

She was reaching for the bell again when a thump and a muffled curse from somewhere inside announced the imminent arrival of the proprietor.

The door opened, just a crack, jerked to a halt by a rusty safety chain. Brown eyes blinked at her from the gloom. 'What?'

Big on customer service, aren't they?

'My name's Judith, erm, Rockerfeller,' she improvised. 'Biotech Industries Limited. I'm interested in your current line of research.'

'Not for sale,' he muttered, as if he'd said it too many times already, and moved to close the door.

Jude had seen that coming. She hurled her full weight against the door. His determination and hers collided through the flimsy wood, stopping it dead. Pain flowered in her shoulder.

'I'm really very interested,' she repeated, fixing him with what she hoped was a commanding stare, 'in your work.'

He rubbed at his forehead for a moment, as if hoping she was a delusion that would be massaged away. She was starting to get the impression that she'd woken him up, and he wasn't exactly a morning person.

'Look, Ms Rockerfeller – like I'm going to believe that one. It's not for sale. What're you going to do, force me to sign the papers?'

'No. But there are some people out there who'd be happy to do exactly that. In fact, they're not even likely to bother with paperwork. And they're going to be here any second, so I suggest you allow me inside, so I can stop them.'

I have no idea how, of course, but . . .

The brown-eyed youth blinked a couple of times, and took half a step back.

That relaxed the pressure on the door just enough to give her an opening. She stepped forward into the door, putting all her weight behind the movement, and the chain tore free from the doorframe. The door hit the wall and bounced back at her, hard, adding a third shoulder bruise to her collection.

'Ah,' he said, scratching his unshaven chin as he regarded the broken chain. 'Well, since you've made your point so forcefully, you'd better come in.'

The hallway was brief and smelled of damp and acetone. Another door opened into a scruffy office, containing a badly upholstered armchair, a coffee machine and a lopsided ply-board desk.

Following her gaze to the crumpled sleeping bag underneath it, the supposed biotech genius went red and kicked the telltale item quickly out of sight.

'I'm not supposed to sleep on the premises,' he muttered, eyes downcast like a naughty schoolboy. 'Business lease. But I get the feeling you won't be telling any tales on me, huh?'

'Looking at this place, I wouldn't know where to start.'

He must have been about thirty, she decided, as he backed

unsteadily into the light. Plump, red-eyed, tired and clumsy with intoxication. Drink? No, drugs, most likely. Pupils still dilated, hands a little shaky as he cleared paperwork from a chair for her, more nervous than polite.

No wonder he didn't know what to make of her. He probably wasn't even sure she was real.

'What's your name?'

'Martin,' he said, with a shrug, as if to diminish its importance.

'All right, Martin –'

And that was when he stepped back, into the fragile glow of an emergency light, and she knew exactly who he was. The hard line of his jaw, the brown eyes that would soon be hollow and cold with disappointment as the world he gave his discovery to as a free gift snatched it, laughed in his face, and forgot him.

'– Harchak, isn't it?'

He blinked.

'Sorry, I've just realised –'

Yeah, what are you going to say, Jude?

'– that we've met before. Somewhere. You really wouldn't remember.'

'No,' he said, with that look her mother used to give her after the first dose of lithium of the day took effect. 'I'll bet I wouldn't.'

No time to worry about reassuring him. What to do, where to start?

'To begin with, I think we should take a look in the lab.'

Which would be the heavily reinforced door behind the desk, the one plastered with BIOHAZARD signs. Bet he takes those down when someone comes for the rent.

Martin frowned.

'Is that going to cause some kind of problem for you, Martin?'

'Are you a biologist?'

Jude bit her lip. 'Not exactly.'

'So how are you going to know what you're looking at? I could show you any old crap. Petroleum jelly. The mould from my coffee cup. And you'd sign up to buy it.'

Jude sighed. This just wasn't right. People were supposed to be grateful when you came hurtling through space and time to save them. All right, she didn't expect medals, but at least they shouldn't threaten to con you.

'Look,' she admitted, lowering herself onto the broad arm of the nearest chair. 'I wasn't exactly straight with you before.'

'No shit,' he muttered, more disappointed than surprised. 'Look. I'm just not in the mood for this. I've already been raided by the Biological Regulatory Authority and the police this week. There are no drugs in the lab. I'll give you my private stash if you'll just go. There's nothing else here of value.'

'That depends on how you look at it. I'm not here to steal from you, Martin. But any minute now, you're going to get some visitors who do plan to take your life's work – and to kill you, too, probably. And they won't even need to use the door. I suggest you take me to wherever your valuable research is, so we can keep an eye on it, and wait for them to show up.'

Martin fumbled behind him, found a coffee mug, gulped at the contents. From the expression on his face, they didn't quite measure up to expectations.

'This,' he mumbled, 'is about the worst scam I have ever heard.'

'That's reassuring. I've never considered myself the criminal type.'

Slamming the mug back onto the desk, he managed, 'These guys who are going to turn up . . .'

'Are big and bad. Oh, and they teleport. Kind of.'

He blinked.

'Did I use the right word? Appearing and disappearing out of thin air?'

'Considering that we're in the heart of the film industry here,' Martin muttered, producing a key from his pocket, 'you came to the wrong office with this spiel. Take it next door, you could make a fortune.'

Jude managed a thin smile. 'Convince you, and I get to save the world as I know it. Which is far from perfect, I admit, but it has to beat what Schrader and his buddies are planning.'

His lips moved. Echoing the name.

'You've heard of him.'

'He phoned.' Martin turned abruptly, sweeping paperwork away to reveal a crude and dusty answering machine. 'Lots of times.'

Of course he did. Rational, by the book Schrader – who can pop back here any time he likes, of course. He'd have tried all the less disruptive approaches. Reported back in between each one, filled in all the paperwork. Violence and theft would be the last resort.

The squeal of rewinding tape, sharp enough to set her teeth on edge. 'So what exactly did he say?'

Martin hit a key and a complaining screech of tape became Schrader's voice, tinny and distorted. '– regarding funding for your research. Please do return my call this time, Martin. Your work is extraordinary, and I'm sure we can reach an arrangement that will benefit both of us.'

He pressed another key, cutting off the terminal bleep. The silence was startling.

Jude frowned at him in the dusty light. 'Why didn't you return his calls, Martin?'

The young man's gaze flickered around the unkempt

room, as if collecting evidence to support his statement. But in the end, all he said was, 'Why should I?'

None of my business anyway. Time's moving on –

'The lab. Let's go.'

She expected more resistance, more time-wasting and persuasion. But that last question seemed to have knocked the fight out of him. Blank faced, Martin moved round the desk and fumbled the key into the lock.

'Me first,' she said, as he reached to open the door.

'There's a lot of delicate –'

'I know that.'

'You can't touch –'

'I know that too. Now get out of my way.'

Cowed, Martin stepped back to allow her through.

More steps, only six of them this time. White walls, white ceiling, the smell of bleach overlaying decay. The set for a mad scientist movie, all brushed metal and glass. Mostly empty, she noticed. Looks like he really was raided. A pile of dog-eared receipts with official stamps, probably to account for whatever they took. Maybe I'm too late, maybe his research is already impounded or destroyed, maybe he didn't have copies . . .

And maybe there was something else she was overlooking. The striplight glare already glinting on flasks and tubes and the polished fronts of cabinets, though she hadn't switched on the lights and she hadn't seen Martin do it either.

And then figures moved in the shadows, and she realised they were there, all three of them. Waiting.

Great idea, Jude. Just walk straight into an ambush.

'This is it, isn't it?' she breathed, trying, and failing, to keep an eye on all of them simultaneously. 'This is the first, illegal, gene-clinic. This is what you came to destroy.'

'Destroy?' DiFlorian sneered.

'"Take possession of" would be closer,' Little Miss said,

moving back from the bench she'd been listlessly examining. 'After all, no gene-clinics, no ReTracers. Even the Government isn't that stupid.'

'You do surprise me.'

'Jude,' the third ReTracer said, stepping forward into the blue glow of a monitor screen. 'It doesn't have to be like this. You're one of us, for God's sake. Join us.'

'Well. Schrader. Wondered how long it would be before you showed up. If you're supposed to be the surprise twist, you're pretty damn predictable.'

He tossed his head, blond fringe flopping in a manner that was probably supposed to be sexy and commanding. He looked plumper, and there was a slight scar on one temple that hadn't been there before. Future-Schrader? she wondered absently. Or uber-Schrader, the sum total of all Schrader-ness from all periods of his life?

'I should have told you what you were,' he admitted, without making much of an effort to sound remorseful. 'But then we didn't know ourselves until fairly –'

Swallowing bile, Jude retorted, 'Until you threw me out of a window, you mean?'

He spread his hands in half-hearted apology. 'Now, now, Jude. What's a little defenestration between friends?'

She was too winded – or too worried – to find a come-back line. Instead, she stepped back to take a real look around to supplement the quick scan for danger she'd taken as she entered.

It wasn't a big operation. Or particularly well-equipped. You didn't have to be an expert to tell that. But it was definitely a gene lab. Big refrigerators labelled with typed notes, names and dates. Centrifuge, microscope, analysis machines of some kind. A little neat for the white heat of scientific progress, surfaces dull with a layer of dust. No one had worked down here for a while; maybe even before the raid this week.

He must still have the notes; the potential, at least. Or they wouldn't be here.

'Oh hell,' Martin sighed, jolting down the stairs behind her. 'How did all you people get in here?'

Jude glanced back at him, deadpan. 'I hate to say "I told you so", but . . .'

He shook his head. Clinging to rational explanations. 'If you're the police, I surrender. If you're another hallucination, then remind me to engineer a cut-off time into my next batch of dope, and go back to hell where you belong.'

'Get him down here,' Schrader said, without even looking at him.

Little Miss Prim smiled, tilting her hips a little in invitation, and beckoned him further into the lab.

'Run,' Jude told him. 'Now.'

He wouldn't. She knew that. Not with everything he cared about down here, vulnerable to these hallucinatory strangers. But she said it anyway.

Martin looked from her to Schrader and back, and slouched down the last two steps into the lab.

'You people, right,' he said, after clearing his throat. 'I know my Freud. You're some kind of manifestation of my inner paranoia, aren't you?'

'Actually,' Jude told him, 'these delightful people are what's going to happen if you don't complete the research you're doing here.'

Schrader blinked, a 'Didn't you get that the wrong way round?' look crumpling his mouth, narrowing his eyes. But then, he never had been smart.

Martin frowned too. To give him his due, he was very good at it. 'It's too hard,' he slurred. 'These days. No money. Got raided last week. They didn't find the good stuff, but the harassment, you know? And too much dope, I guess. It's just too hard.'

'I know,' Jude murmured. Though she didn't, not really. 'I know. But what you're doing here is very important. World-changing. I think you know that.'

'Sure,' DiFlorian said. 'If you're a body purist. A fascist by any other name. If you want a world where everyone's the same, everyone's "perfect" –but by whose definition?'

'Yours, I presume. If you get control of biotech at its earliest stages, only give it to those you consider fit. Or unfit.' Anger flared in Jude, fed by garbled memories of late nights in Club Andro, strange and ecstatic creatures flitting in the shadows. 'And you say I'm a fascist. What are your parameters going to be? Who deserves biotech, in your brave new world? And who's going to get it, whether they want it or not?'

Schrader tossed his head. He probably wasn't used to being disagreed with. 'The alternative is the world we grew up in. A world where everyone has to follow fashion. Obsessed by the skin-deep. Everyone has to have the latest body, the latest face. Is that right, or fair? You were lucky, Jude, you look pretty much okay even without bioteching –'

'You really know how to flatter a girl, don't you?'

'But what if you didn't match up to the accepted norm? Imagine the pressure. The whispers. Isn't it better to keep biotech for the sick and the diseased, the ones who really need it, than to allow criminals to coin new identities –'

'Sheesh,' Martin muttered, following the conversation round the room with those wide, startled eyes. 'I'm hallucinating ethical philosophy.'

'Yeah,' Little Miss growled. 'You should really take a holiday.'

Jude shook her head. 'You don't give a damn about anyone but yourselves and your bloody superhuman powers. The only people you'd be "keeping" the technology for are yourselves. And what you need,' to Martin, backing unsteadily up the steps now, 'isn't a holiday. You need to carry on where you left off. Finish the research, distribute it as widely as you can. Share the secret. They'll rip you off, and you will get pretty bitter about that – but you were never that interested in big business anyway. You just want to change the world. And that's exactly what you're going to do.'

You're going to give me a little time with the woman I love, who wouldn't be a woman at all if it wasn't for your dope-filled experimentation. A little time being better than no time.

Which is about what I have left here.

Schrader took a step forward. 'It's unfortunate, Jude, but we just can't allow that to happen.'

She returned his stare. 'Well, yes, Schrader. That is unfortunate.'

Mainly because I have no idea how to stop you.

I should never have listened to Warner, that's for sure. Should have joined the Ferrymen while I had the chance. Moved in with mummy dearest and started imagining towers into existence. Should have stayed Adrift.

Of course. And how did I end up Adrift in the first place?

I died. My physical body died.

'Martin. Why don't you wait upstairs for a moment? Let me and the Hitler Youth here sort this out between ourselves.'

Miss Handbag blew air through her teeth. 'There's no need for that sort of association. GenoBond has no racial or –'

'Now, Martin.'

Blinking in panic, he backed up the last two steps and closed the door on them. The click of the latch echoed strangely off the tiled walls, the glistening metal cabinets.

Schrader regarded her sourly across the heaps of jumbled equipment. 'If he makes a run for it while we're down here . . .'

'Fat Boy's not going anywhere,' DiFlorian muttered. 'His whole life's work is here.'

Jude turned her attention to the bench in front of her.

Yeah, I really should have paid more attention in Chemistry, too. When I get all this over with, I'm going back to evening classes, to patch up all these irritating little holes in my education. It's not like I won't have the time, because, after all, I won't have a job after I break Mr Warner's nose . . .

Little Miss Handbag was looking at her. 'Let me get this straight. You want to work things out?'

That flask there should do the trick. If she could only get to it.

'Well, you know me. Always the accommodating type.'

Schrader pulled a face.

'No, really. I mean, what's the point? The way I see it, you people have everything worked out. Control bioteching, control people's desires. No more nasty incidents with people convinced they're a llama trapped in the body of a man. The way you see things, you're making everybody happy, healthy and compliant to the New World Order.'

'Jude –'

'And that's all very well.' One more step; no, another, just be sure it was well within reach. 'But the thing is –'

'Stop.'

Schrader, abruptly still, frozen, his gaze fixed to her hand as she leaned forward, oh so casually, to rest against the bench. 'Whatever you're going to try, don't.'

'Sorry guys.'

Her fingers closed around the glass flask, flipping it up into the air. Little Miss was going for the ugly-looking revolver holstered under the arm, but it was too late for that. The flask clipped the edge of a ceiling beam and shattered, broken glass and fumes spiralling in an expanding cloud. Schrader, closest to her, fell back, choking. For a moment, he was there, reaching for her *and also on the ground, clawing at his raw throat, spitting blood*

And then the air conditioning kicked in, a long, laboured

rattling that barely thinned the white and spiralling fumes. *And the smoke of her burning*, some garbled memory chimed in, *goes up for ever and ever . . .*

And she just stood there, listening to three people dying.

Not dying, really. I mean, they're dead the same way I'm dead, and here I am, happy as a sandboy. Whatever a sandboy is. And they're criminals, killers, I mean, how did I end up dead in the first place?

I'm still killing human beings.

I'm going to break a lot more than just Warner's nose when I get home.

The air conditioning was making headway now, clearing a small and continually threatened space immediately below the out-take vent. For a moment, there was just the machinery hum.

Then DiFlorian stumbled forward into clean air, brushing ineffectually at the acid splashes on her sleeve. 'That was so childish. I don't know what you thought you'd achieve –'

'Bang, bang,' Jude said, finally allowing herself a smile. 'You're dead.'

It wasn't a thing you could see, as such. It was more a feeling, an unconscious reading of tiny clues. The thinness, the fading, the brittle look in their eyes. The way they looked at each other, the widening of pupils, the terrible, laboured slowness of their realisation. Oh, and the way she could see right through the trailing edge of Miss Handbag's skirt.

No wonder Doctor Gene'n'stein there thought we were hallucinations. We're worse than that. We're ghosts. Revenants. Beings caught outside their own time.

Tossing that overgrown fringe back out of his eyes, Schrader pushed DiFlorian aside and kept coming.

'Time,' he muttered, 'to see if you really can kill the dead.'

Jude just smiled.

'Don't you feel it, Schrader?'

She could. Exactly as she'd felt it in the street, as she looked back at her own dead body. The swirling, the vertigo, the beginning of the end.

One moment Schrader was there, reaching for her; then the floor gave way beneath him, and he was falling.

Instinctively, Jude jumped back, cursing herself for not having anticipated the one small drawback to the plan. The fact that she, also being somewhat dead, might get sucked in too.

The wall was at her back, and, even if there'd been room to run, it wouldn't have helped her. The whirlwind that had once been the floor was expanding too fast. Jagged fragments of time spinning like an exploding mirror, reflections still trapped behind the glass as it came apart. Sucking DiFlorian and Little Miss down like spiders in a bath tub, plucking at her toes, tugging at the hem of her jeans – and then vertigo engulfed her, and, for the last time, she was falling.

SIXTEEN

Adrift

It was going to end the way it had started.

Four ReTracers, all Adrift. All points of reference wiped by their deaths, each lost in the cracks between the moments of their lives. She'd been here before, of course, and found a way out. But it had been her life passing her by in fragments and glimpses, hers alone: now the flashes of time flickering past were the lives of strangers, the men and women trapped there cried out for people she'd never known, and she wasn't sure her luck was going to hold.

The others were trying to save themselves, just as she'd done. Lunging and clutching at whatever passed, at the slivers of reality that danced between them like snowflakes, groping for the detritus of past and future, slashing their naked hands on the edges of time. Some of those lives flashing by were theirs. All they needed was the right moment to jump to, and they were safe.

Looking back, she saw DiFlorian catch a hold on the jagged edge of a place she didn't even recognise, orange-skied and whirlwinded by dust. She looked into it like a mirror, just for a moment; then she had to accept that she didn't belong there, and the fragment twisted from her hand and vanished into the dark.

It was a pity she was never going to get to report back to Warner, the bastard. He'd have loved this story. Well, Mr Warner, once I'd traced the minions of evil to the secret laboratory, I killed them – and then, as the laws of physics seem to require of dead ReTracers, we all ended up Adrift . . .

Maybe one day someone would realise that it wasn't a

mistake but a higher level, a short-cut through time, a new way to play the game. The game that Schrader and friends were playing – that she'd so recently learned – whether they realised it or not. A whole new level to be exploited, a whole new way to waste official time and money.

Not to mention your own. Spending your life going backwards, revising the opening chapters and forgetting to live the middle and the end. An evolutionary dead end.

I want to go home.

Even above the wind-rush, she could hear Miss Handbag swearing. Colourful vocabulary, bet she hadn't learned that in the manicurist's . . .

But she was way behind, way above, barely visible through the flicker of fragmented realities. She was irrelevant. It was Schrader who was the problem.

He was catching up with her.

Not that he was doing anything, physically, but this place didn't seem to work by the normal rules. No, he was definitely accelerating, and any moment now . . .

Jude reached out and snatched at the jagged slice of time at her right hand. Solid. Cold. Flickering with trapped movement. A jumble of ferns and grey sky and women's laughter. It would only take a moment's concentration, a moment's will, and she could tumble through it like Alice through the rabbit hole, thrown stunned and trembling into an alien world.

Not yet.

Averting her eyes from the shimmering summer's day she held between forefinger and thumb, she hurled it at Schrader.

It smacked flat against his crooked knee and shattered, spilling shredded hysteria into the up-draught like shards of glass, bright and brittle. Several gashed his face on the way, but he only blinked away the blood – yellow blood, releasing the scent of roses and the cries of fledgling birds on a warm spring day – and reached for her.

She ducked. Grabbed another fragment out of the nothingness and hit him again. A fragment of pain and someone screaming abuse in a language she'd never heard before. Nice shot. Right in the chest. Must have hurt.

But he understood the game now. He lifted one hand, waiting for something to drift within reach. Then lunged at the next flicker of light, caught it, hurled it like a discus. Flames danced across its surface, and Jude knew instinctively that it wasn't going to be a good place to end up, dead or undead.

She leant back into the airstream, and it hit a passing fragment before it hit her, shattering a pseudo-operatic chorus of monks in a shower of screams. Diamond-edged shrapnel flowered between them, pushing them apart. She drew her knees up to her chest, trying to make herself a smaller target. Schrader was shouting, curses ripped from his mouth by the wind, as he lunged, fingers clawing for her eyes.

Little Miss Handbag slammed into him from above. A tangle of legs, arms and immaculate stockings laddering under Schrader's nails, pawing and scrambling like an erotic carving, locked together as they fell and fell and fell–

And, looking down, Jude saw the light and knew that they weren't going to fall forever.

Schrader was screaming – screaming into the light, the nuclear-white thunderflash brilliance, and all she could think of was helicopters and music and the world in flames –

This is the end, beautiful friend, Warner, I'll be back to haunt you, I swear –

No safety or surprise, the end, dying, finally, and still all my brain has to offer is old movies –

I'll never look into your eyes . . .

Hurtling up at her out of the dark, a half-familiar face frowned concern at her from the brittle surface of a slice of time.

Again.

EPILOGUE

If she thought back, just a few seconds further, she ought to be able to remember the moment the bodies actually hit the ground.

Because there they were, only four paces away. Just a glimpse of splayed limbs and crushed torsos flowering blood onto a dirty pavement. People pressing in around it now, coming out of the office block foyer or peeling away from the kerbside stalls to gather and stare. Not move, not help; just stare. As if that was a valid response, as if their rapt attention was a necessary part of the process.

'Mass executive suicide,' one of the stallholders muttered, rolling his eyes theatrically to the iron-grey heavens. 'For goodness' sake. Thought we'd done with that when most of them moved out to the Hursts.'

'And who's responsible for the clearing-up?' a man in a greasy apron growled. 'I got a living to make. People don't buy fajitas if they have to step over bodies to get to them.'

'You could put 'em all in the fillings,' the woman at his elbow suggested, triggering a ripple of nervous laughter. 'Seems a pity to waste them.'

Jude blinked.

What the hell am I doing here?

A thin trickle of blood ran from beneath an impact-scuffed leather handbag and down into the gutter beside her.

Didn't that look familiar?

A hand fell on her shoulder and she turned. Remembering.

All of it. Warner, Miss Leather Shoes and Handbag, her mother and the tower, Little East Bankside, a hotel room, a river of death, a hole in time and always falling . . .

The young man with his hand on her shoulder took a step back, brown eyes widening. The eyes of the young man on the Ulti-Mall sliproad. The rest taller, broader across the shoulders, neatly honed in the way that only a new incarnation could be, before good living and bad living and living in general had screwed it up.

'Fitch,' she said, and tears welled behind her eyelids.

The thin mouth parted. A smile. 'You haven't called me that for a while.'

Nothing to be said to that, only questions. She seized his hand, swinging him away from the thinning crowd. 'Let's get away from here.'

And then she saw them. Just faces in the crowd, as blank and puzzled as she knew her own must be. Schrader, frowning down on a lost shoe as if some part of him knew it belonged on his foot. Little Miss. DiFlorian, even, rubbing her eyes as if to scour away the sight of a body too familiar and yet undeniably not her.

This is what she told me on the roof at the Pigsty. Trying to give her the vital clue. 'Unless we can find a world where we weren't born us.'

Where someone else inherited my rogue gene and learned to travel time at will, and died for it, and I . . .

And I am someone else entirely.

Someone who's finally free of the temptation to remake their life continually, to keep polishing every moment until it's artifically glittering and perfect. Someone who just lives, like everyone else, making mistakes and handling the consequences and hopefully doing a little better next time.

'Jude . . .?'

Concern rumpled Fitch's unfamiliar face; his arm closed around her shoulders, a gesture so intimate she almost shivered.

Across the crowd, Schrader met her gaze, a flicker of

recognition in his eyes. Then he nodded very slightly, as if thanking her for something, and turned away.

Stepping back, further into Fitch's embrace, Jude whispered, 'Yeah. Definitely time to go.'

He didn't let go until they were a full three blocks away, striding through scattered bystanders towards the distant ruins of Marble Arch – mostly scaffolding, rickety metalwork and warning signs.

As she turned back to see if anyone had taken charge of the tragedy yet, not-exactly-Fitch said, 'You're in trouble, aren't you?'

'Yes,' she spluttered, hysteria rising at the sudden realisation that she probably was.

He just nodded. 'What can I do?'

Jude leant into the warmth, the weight of his embrace. Good question.

'Jude?'

'Listen . . .' What to call this stranger/lover/friend? 'Honey. It's like this.'

You're surely not going to tell him the truth?

Whatever that is.

'There's, ah, a kind of memory loss that affects ReTracers. Wipes out chunks of recent memory. I mean, I remember who I am and everything, but I don't know how I got here today, and the last few hours, well, days . . .' She searched that immaculate face for clues. 'Longer, maybe.'

He bit his lip. 'You do remember taking me in for the switchback?'

Jude shook her head.

'You did agree. I wouldn't have done it if –'

'I know. I mean, I know that I should have. I know I must have. Hell, you know what I mean.'

Somewhere under a strange face, a familiar Fitch smiled.

'So. How long ago did you, erm . . .?'

He took her by the elbow, as if afraid she was about to stumble. 'Jude. I think you should see a doctor. A specialist.' Inspiration sparked in his eyes. 'If this is something that affects ReTracers, maybe I should take you in to GenoBond?'

'No. That would be a bad mistake. A fatal mistake. All I need to be filled in on what I've missed. Oh, and then we need to pack, and get the hell out of here. Ever thought about going north?'

Fitch looked vaguely alarmed. 'Manchester?'

'I was thinking more like Helsinki.'

'Ah,' he said. 'That kind of trouble. Come on. We can talk about . . . what you don't remember, on the way.'

Jude squinted back up the street. The last few ghouls were giving up, curiosity sated, and fading back into the crowd. People from inside the office block were taking charge of the bodies, ordering men in caretaker's overalls to bundle them in plastic and move them inside. Somehow, their interest didn't surprise her, but she couldn't quite remember why.

'Who was it that jumped?' Fitch asked softly. 'Someone you knew?'

Jude turned away, forcing herself to smile. 'No. No one I really knew at all.'

ABOUT HONNO

Honno Welsh Women's Press was set up in 1986 by a group of women who felt strongly that women in Wales needed wider opportunities to see their writing in print and to become involved in the publishing process. Our aim is to publish books by, and for, women of Wales, and our brief encompasses fiction, poetry, children's books, autobiographical writing and reprints of classic titles in English and Welsh.

Honno is registered as a community co-operative and so far we have raised capital by selling shares at £5 a time to over 350 interested women all over the world. Any profit we make goes towards the cost of future publications. We hope that many more women will be able to help us in this way. Shareholders' liability is limited to the amount invested, and each shareholder, regardless of the number of shares held, will have her say in the company and a vote at the AGM. To buy shares or to receive further information about forthcoming publications, please write to Honno:

'Ailsa Craig'
Heol y Cawl
Dinas Powys
Bro Morgannwg
CF64 4AH.